Pagan Love Story

Pagan Love Story

by

Anonymous

Pink Plum Press
Sagaponack, NY 11962

Cover design by Constance von Collande.

ISBN   0-9707989-03

Pink Plum Press
PO Box 498
Sagaponack, NY 11962

Pagan Love Story

It was a warm Friday afternoon in late June. I was in the store on my knees, feather-dusting the canned tomatoes and lost in my daydreams when I noticed a woman's perfume. My eyes followed my nose. I looked up and there was a Lady standing over me. She looked familiar, although I could not remember ever having seen her. Certainly I had never been in the presence of such dramatic beauty.

Her face had an angelic conformity of feature, but there was a demon looking out from her large, dark eyes. Her nose was delicate, her chin was strong and her mouth was wide and sensual. She had a mane of thick, wavy hair and flawlessly smooth skin. There was nothing subtle about her womanhood. She wore a starched white shirt, tailored to flatter her breasts, and stretch riding pants that hugged her every contour. Since I was kneeling, the Mystery was level with my eyes. I dared not stare. I took a quick look then cast my eyes on her boots, which were straight-laced and came up her calves. Her perfume was an elegant bouquet, an air of luxury, potency and indulgence. I detected an animal note in the bass, a cryptic scent that beckoned to a living temple of flesh.

I felt lost in her presence.

"Hmm!" She gave a short hum of impatience and

tapped her foot on the floor. "Wake up, boy." She snapped her fingers. I noticed she wore an unusual ring: a gold snake coiling around her left pinky peered at me through a ruby eye.

"Can I help you, Madam?"

"Where is Edgar?" Her voice was controlled, firm yet feminine, with a clear musical tone and a distinctly patrician quaver.

"Edgar retired at the end of last season, Madam. I'm the new clerk here."

"You're just a boy," she said coldly, with obvious disappointment.

"Sorry, Madam," I said. I introduced myself.

"That sounds more like something to eat than a name," she laughed. "I am Lady Ketchener."

Of course she looked familiar. Burke Ketchener, a blue-blooded playgirl, one of Norbury's many illustrious residents, was on the cover of *Bagatelle* recently.

I rose to my feet. Even though she was two inches shorter than I, I felt dwarfed by her. I bowed and begged her to forgive my stupidity and slowness. I told her I was honored to meet her. She made no sign of accepting my apologies or my compliments. Instead she gave me a sharp look that let me know I was talking too much. She handed me a list. She said she would be spending the summer in Norbury and was going to depend on me to order these items and keep them in stock. My predecessor apparently did as much.

Self-satisfied, yet starved for attention, Burke Ketchener had the makings of a tough customer. But I found her intensely compelling. My heart fluttered. I wanted to see her satisfied. I told her it would be my pleasure to serve her.

"We shall see!" she said with an imposing sneer.

When she left, I felt weak and near breathless, yet energized in a way I had never known before.

Ever since I learned the alphabet, I was drawn to write.

The quiet, genteel hill country in northwestern Connecticut hosted an educated population with a good number of writers among them. It seemed a fitting place for me. Soon after college, I found employment at Emerson's Village Grocery in Norbury. The job didn't pay much, but the hours were short, the work undemanding. I thought it would leave me time and a proper frame-of-mind to pursue the Muse.

Mister Emerson referred me to a middle-aged widow who rented rooms in one of the large Victorian houses on Main Street. Mrs Gooden was a doughy woman who walked with a cane. At first she was suspicious and reserved. But when she heard I was a writer, she offered me coffee and fresh-baked cinnamon buns.

"Writers make the best boarders," she said. "Quiet as mice."

I felt that the Muse demanded I accept a humble station in life, that I submit myself to that Goddess's unpredictable guiding light, and that I discipline myself to the daily grind necessary for honing the writing craft. My first novel, a romantic comedy about a young man who prevails in spite of his naivete, proved more difficult to write than I had anticipated. To enhance my verbal creativity when I bogged down, I repeated a little prayer dedicating myself to the Mother Goddess.

To You, the Writing in my Flesh, I dedicate myself.
Goddess of Love, who brings joy and woe, I am
your instrument. My work is not my own but
yours.

After a while, my head would clear. The words, sentences and paragraphs would come naturally.

That evening, after my encounter with Burke Ketchener, I went to the library and found the back issue of *Bagatelle*. For all the magazine's literary affectations, glossy pages and haughty advertisements, it was a gossip rag. Like a supermarket tabloid, it resorted to people's lowest common denominator. Sex, after all, sells. I devoured the story from start to finish.

Burke Briddle Ketchener was the daughter of Seraphina Burke Peck and Jason Briddle. The Pecks were one of Connecticut's oldest and richest families who owned a good part of Litchfield County including Lavender Hill Farm, a two thousand acre estate which boasted of being New England's most distinguished horse farm and boarding stable. Jason Briddle was the co-founder of *Briddle and Baines,* the Wall Street brokerage firm. When Burke was five, Seraphina and Jason died in an avalanche on a ski trip in Switzerland. Young Burke, left an orphan with a sizeable fortune, was raised in Boston by her maternal aunt.

The piece provided an intimate profile of the socialite as a young woman, including pictures of her at nineteen with Kelman Straub the notorious movie actor, at twenty-one with Armando Peirrera the ballet dancer, and at twenty-three with Dario Borghini the Italian prince and race-car driver whom she married. Three months after the ceremony, Borghini was killed when his car flew out of control on a mountain road. Her second marriage was to Barton Ketchener, the youngest member of the House of Lords. The attractive couple were the darlings of gossip columnists. By appearances it was a match made in heaven. Nevertheless, there were rumors of problems, involving infidelities on both sides.

As Lady Ketchener, her lifestyle was truly extravagant. She dined with heads of state and the living legends of art and entertainment. She had a flamboyant sense of *noblesse oblige*. There were pictures of her in Ethiopia feeding starving refugees, in New York City being held in jail cell for taking part in a demonstration against police brutality, in Nicaragua covered with mud helping hurricane victims, and in a Latvian pediatric ward nursing children whose cancers were believed to have come from the unconscionable dumping of toxic waste.

The article implied that her humanitarian streak and her missions of mercy, well-publicized as they were, were facets of her megalomania. Her excessive self-admiration demanded an audience to confirm it.

There was an exposé of her secret life of leisure, extravagance and dissipation. Last year, her marriage to Lord Ketchener fell apart. The author had an exclusive interview with a close but unnamed personal friend of the family who revealed that Lord Ketchener sued for divorce after he found Burke with one of the stable boys.

I went home to my little room at Mrs Gooden's. Moved by a force over which I had no control, I lay on the bed with my eyes closed. I visualized Lady Ketchener as I had seen her that day and summoned her scent to mind. I imagined myself as her stable boy, entirely at her service. The love welled up in me and overflowed into a flannel hand towel.

Through the month of July, Lady Ketchener called every morning. She coolly listed her order without an extraneous remark and often spoke more quickly than I could write. When I begged her pardon so I could catch up, she huffed impatiently and continued speaking a jot slower but with obvious exasperation in her voice.

Around midday, her driver, a gentleman from the old school named Jasper, would come to collect what she had ordered. I took special care to insure her satisfaction. Even when everything was just as she ordered it, she was not pleased. She would usually call back in the afternoon to complain about some imaginary oversight or to blame me for circumstances beyond my control, such as a change in a product's packaging or its lack of availability in a size that suited her.

She was temperamental, distant and contemptuous.

Despite her exacting attitude, I looked forward to hearing her voice every morning. I was disappointed if she did not call to complain in the afternoon. I rehearsed my apologies. In an attempt to keep her on the line, I would try to make small talk, commenting on the weather, the traffic or items of local interest. She would reply with a peevish grumble and abruptly end the conversation, expressing her hope that I would do better tomorrow. I assured her I would.

One day I ventured to tell her that I admired her for the good work she did.

"It is not every beautiful woman who has a sense of justice," I said. "The magazine was unfair. After all, you do sacrifice your comfort, and at times have risked your life, trying to bring attention to suffering people."

There was an icy silence on the line.

I was instantly sorry I had said such a personal thing. I apologized.

"That will be all," she said simply and hung up.

I spent the remainder of the day furious with myself for being so stupid. What if she decided to shop elsewhere?

But the following morning she came in person, perfectly coiffed, dressed in expensive sports clothes and Italian sunglasses. My senses perked up in her presence. I greeted her with the greatest warmth and respect. She behaved as if she had never seen me or spoken to me before. She read her list and I picked the items from the shelves. I managed to have everything just as she wanted it. I carried her purchases to her car. She drove off without so much as a nod of appreciation.

From then on she would call in the morning and pick up in person. What had happened to Jasper? I dared not ask. Alternately hot-tempered and cold, she was as mean as she was beautiful; her irritation with me seemed to grow daily. I thought her more lovely every time I saw her.

One day toward the end of August she came in early. Rain had curtailed her riding. I had not finished collecting her order.

In a lather because she had to wait, she tapped the mud from her boots onto the floor and drummed impatiently on the counter with the end of her crop. "Like so many little people, you're incompetent," she snapped. "You've earned your lowly lot in life."

I imagined she loathed me. Whether because of this apparent aversion or despite it, my acts of worship became more frequent. Not only would I discharge my passion before I went to sleep, but invariably in the night I would dream of her and wake, powerless to control my pull in her direction.

She meant the world to me and I was sure she could not even remember my name. If I died tomorrow, her concern would be to whom did she have to speak to make sure her favorite jams and jellies were in stock.

On the Friday before the Labor Day Weekend as I put her groceries into the back of her car, she carelessly mentioned that she was looking for a houseboy and asked if I was interested in applying for the position.

Was I!

The interview was set for Monday at three in the afternoon. My prayers seemed to have been answered. I was tingling with excitement. But was this dreadful anxiety what I really wanted? I could hardly eat or sleep. I stayed up late Sunday night working on my novel, burning candles and pledging myself to the Goddess of Love.

I woke late on Monday. The weather was splendid, deep blue skies, golden sunshine, a light dry breeze with a few puffy clouds. I was on fire. I bathed and put on my only dress pants, a clean white shirt and shiny shoes. I did not have a car. I called the village taxi.

In Norbury everyone minded everyone else's business. When Herbie the driver heard where he was taking me, he asked what cause I had to go to Lavender Hill Farm. I already understood that circumspection was part of the position for which I was applying. I did not answer his question, but remarked on the fine day. Herbie said it was a taste of the upcoming fall. We both agreed that the fall was our favorite season.

We drove west along Twin Ponds Highway to Fresh Meadows Road. About two miles up Fresh Meadows Road the hills were rolling green. Then I saw the fences, fresh-painted white and marked with the Lavender Hill Farm emblem, intertwined script L, H and F. Horses grazed peacefully.

The drive was an alley of maples. The house was a grand old country manor with several recent additions, all surrounded by extensive flower gardens. I asked Herbie to drop me around back. My surging blood sounded like a hundred bells inside my head. I swallowed hard and pressed the buzzer at the service entrance.

I was surprised when Lady Ketchener let me in herself. She was wearing her riding togs. She had evidently just come in. There were beads of perspiration on her brow. Her body heat intensified her meaty scent.

She bid me follow her.

We went through a mud room. I saw several pairs of soiled riding boots under the bench. She led me through the kitchen. There were dirty dishes in the sink; the stove looked as if it had not been cleaned in weeks. The dining room was large, the table formal. There were newspapers, magazines, mail and various items of clothing strewn about.

We arrived in a large parlor with huge windows that brought the picturesque country inside. The view went to the distant hills. In the foreground was a meadow with horses nibbling the green grass and swatting flies with their tails.

Lady Ketchener was more moving than any scenery. She went to the bar, poured herself a Scotch, lit a cigarette and sat down in a high-backed armchair. She did not invite me to sit, but instead looked me up and down very boldly. I felt nervous and awkward in her presence. Were my pants wrinkled? Was my shirt not tucked-in properly? I tried not to be too obvious as I checked my fly.

She inhaled on her cigarette. "A couple of weeks ago I fired the entire staff," she said, blowing smoke. "the whole bunch of them, the housemaid, my personal maid, the chef, my secretary, the gardener and the driver. I came to the country to relax, not to have people bustling every which way and chatting out of turn. I want to replace them all with one person. He would live here, take care of what needs to be taken care of, and be unobtrusive. Do you think you can handle it?"

I told her I thought cleaning and running errands were easy enough. I had worked as a gardener and a cook and found both enjoyable. Also I had aspirations as a writer. Short social notes would hardly be a problem. I did not have many personal needs or possessions, and while I was not shy, I was quiet.

I looked at her and smiled. I hoped I was making a good impression.

"Don't be so cocky, boy," she said with an edge of displeasure in her voice. "And do I have to tell you? Keep your eyes down in my presence!"

"Sorry, Madam." I moved my gaze to her boots.

"*Sorry* is not good enough. I have the highest standards. My 'sense of justice', as you call it, does not apply to *my* servants. In *my* house, you have no rights. You will not speak unless spoken to. You are at my beck and call around the clock, every day. When I give an order, I want it obeyed like that." She snapped her fingers. "And no questions asked."

I was deflated by her sharpness.

"As you can tell, I don't believe in mincing words. Are you still interested in the job?"

"Oh, yes, Madam."

She softened a bit. "You seem like a good boy, honest, intelligent, hard-working. But you're impertinent. You don't know your place. Do you think you can learn to submit yourself entirely to me?"

"Madam, I have little in the way of personal life. Both my parents are dead; I have no brothers or sisters; my close friends all live in Boston or New York." She tapped her foot impatiently as I went on telling about myself. I tried to hold my tongue, but I was unable. "My position at the grocery is merely to hold my body together while I write. The job is dreadfully boring and for what it pays I would quit in an instant. The only thing that is important to me is my writing. Will there be times when I will be free to write?"

"A writer are you?" she asked. "And what do you write?" I heard derision in her voice.

"Fiction, Madam, or I'm trying anyway."

"What is your story about?"

"It's a farce about love," I began to explain. "A young man meets a woman and —"

She cut me off. "That might be interesting. Or it might not. Unless I tell you otherwise, you are to be in your quarters every night at ten. I want my coffee every morning at eight. Of course you will be on call all night. But what you do in your room, provided it does not disturb me, is up to you. I suggest you become an early riser and learn to stick to a schedule. The best writers do, you know. Everything you write while you are in my house will be open to my examination."

I told her that I would be flattered if she took any interest at all in my work. For a moment she seemed pleased. Then she said, "But that is not what I meant when I said you must belong *entirely* to me. If you want to work for me, you must exist to please me."

Although I clearly heard what she said, I was not sure I understood the implication. "Do you mean —?" I was too embarrassed to finish the question.

"Yes, exactly," she said, reaching out and stroking my leg. "I mean I must own you. You see, I like sex but I tire quickly of men. I don't like having anyone making demands on me. Your complete obedience is the key to my pleasure. If I say I want you, boy, you're there; and if I say I don't, you're not."

I was speechless. I swallowed hard and managed to nod my head, yes.

"I didn't hear you, boy?"

"Yes!"

"Yes, *Madam*!" she corrected me.

"Yes, Madam," I replied

"Good," she said. "Now, of course, before I decide if

17

you are worth training. I have to see what you look like. Please remove your clothing."

It was all so unexpected. Excited, self-conscious, incredulous that she really wanted me to strip, I found myself nearly paralyzed by the audacious request. I fiddled with the top button of my shirt.

"Where is the compliance you promised me?" she snarled. "If I have to tell you twice, you may leave."

Flustered and embarrassed, yet roused to the bone, I showed her how fast I could obey.

Sipping Scotch and blowing smoke, she looked me over. She ordered me to walk up and down, then stand at attention in front of her. I did so. She stubbed out her cigarette and put down her drink. She appraised me very personally with her fine nose. She had me open my mouth so she could see my teeth. She ran her long fingers through my hair, then pulled it to see how much would come out. It hurt and I cried out.

"Don't be such a sissy," she said.

She handled my body as if it were her own. With her soft fingertips and her hard nails, her touch was cool, calculating, instinctive. She seemed to know everything about me, my cravings, my fears. She felt the muscles in my arms and legs. She moved her hand up my leg and explored my genitals. She used the edge of her nails to tickle me just under the tip of my penis where I was most sensitive. I went into a rapture of love. My eagerness to please elevated accordingly. She gathered a few drops of my lubricity on her finger and tasted.

"Not bad," she granted. She leaned forward and took me in her mouth. She made me very aware of her teeth.

"While you are here," she said, "your purpose in life is to learn complete submission to me. Your body is not your own, most especially this, this . . . this *mouse*. A timid little creature for the big she-cat to catch, eh? Yes. How fitting! Mouse! It's also a small, hand-held input device which allows a user to select operations on a computer, isn't it?"

"Yes, Madam!"

She picked up a tailor's tape which was lying on the desk. "Let's see how big *my* mouse is."

She held the tape to my erection.

"Too bad," she said with a cheerless sigh. "Only average."

I was flattened by her remark, but her mouse, wanting desperately to suit her, stretched his head hoping for another measurement. However, she pushed down on my shoulders and said, "Let's see you on all fours, boy."

I obeyed. On my hands and knees in front of her seemed the position I was born to assume.

"Spread," she said, coming around behind me and tapping the inside of my legs with the toe of her boot. I moved my knees apart. She pinched my buttocks. "This is mine," she said. "And this is mine." She poked between my cheeks.

I nodded my agreement. "As you say, Madam."

"Henceforth you will no longer have a name," she went on. "You are my mouse, Lady Ketchener's boy. I am your owner and I have complete power over you, to have, hold, sell, turn away, enjoy, dispose of, judge and punish as I will. Do you understand?"

"Yes, Madam. I understand."

"Good," she said. "At least you seem to have some control of yourself. But I'm not certain you are good enough for me. I don't know how easy it will be to knock that audacity out of you."

"I will apply myself, Madam," I promised. "You won't be disappointed."

"All right. I will try you."

"You mean I'm hired."

"I said you are on trial. I will test your fitness for six weeks."

"When do I start?"

"You already have started."

"But my job at the grocery —"

"I took the liberty of calling Mister Emerson earlier in the week. I talked to him about taking you. I promised to put in a good word for him with the screening committee at the Arcadian Club. He had little chance of getting in without my sponsorship. He was quite grateful. He said his nephew will be happy to replace you at the store, if I decided to give you a place here."

The knowledge that she thought about me and even spoke to Mister Emerson about me made my heart jump. Maybe she *did* feel for me some of what I felt for her.

I asked her about salary and she laughed. "How dare you ask for compensation! You will have food, clothing, a place to sleep and you will be near me. I am an experienced woman. You are just a boy. If anything, you should pay me. And you will, I promise. No, not in money, but with your soul."

"Yes, Madam."

I was still on my knees. She walked around in front of me and turned her behind to my face. She was perfect in her tight riding pants.

She unbuckled her belt, unbuttoned her pants and pulled them down. I saw perfection beyond perfection. Her skin was smooth white; her panties were black silk briefs edged with the finest lace.

"Now, come, show your devotion to your Mistress. Don't hold anything back. Let me see what you can do."

The truth is I had not had much experience. I had had only four girlfriends and they were all very shy. Not sure of what she wanted, I kissed her lightly on the hind cheek. She grunted with irritation. "You must do better than that, boy," she said, pulling her panties down and bending over, offering her bottom to my mouth. "Show me how you much love me!" she commanded as she drove her soft nether region into my face.

Even at its earthiest, her flesh was heavenly sweet. I pressed my tongue and nose into her like a hungry dog and murmured with burning desire. My passion seemed to please her. She purred and began to breathe deeply. The speed of her movements increased and then her buttocks stiffened and clenched in a spasm of pleasure.

She released her hold. I was quite aroused and touched her gently on the lips of her sex with my fingertips, but she pulled away. How quickly the diversion she enjoyed turned to impatience! "Madam is finished!" she said very sternly. "She's not here to amuse you." She pushed my head down, forcing me to lie flat on the floor.

I remained prostrate before her as she pulled up her panties and buttoned her pants. She picked up her drink, lit a cigarette and paced nervously. The sight of her boots, the sound they made on the floor, the smell of the leather had me enthralled. Then she unlooped her belt, which had a silver buckle and a silver tip, and walked around behind me, clicking her tongue and slapping the leather strap lightly against her palm. I was transported by an emotion that combined fear and love, dread and lust.

"You are mine," she said as slid the instep of her boot up my legs and lodged it between my prick and the floor.

A few drops of my male oil oozed onto the toe of her boot. She slid her toe back and buffed the leather against my soft swag. "Whenever, wherever and however I'm moved to touch you, you will welcome me. But you must never, never, never touch me unless I specifically request it. Is that understood?"

I nodded. I begged for forgiveness.

"You need a reminder that you are here to serve me, rather than the other way around."

With her boot toe still pressing against my delicate drupes, she hit me across the left shoulder blade with the silver tip of her belt. The blow broke the skin. She rubbed her hand vigorously over the wound to diffuse the blood. The sensation of heat penetrated me to my marrow. Whatever the physical pain, my emotions were more affected than my flesh. I could not separate bliss from anguish. She was a ruling presence such as I had never known. I was conquered.

I felt I would ejaculate but I instinctively knew I must not do so without her permission. Instead I burst into hysterical tears.

"If you want to be my boy you must be able to take punishment like a man," she said.

She swatted me again on the shoulder. The throbbing physical pain helped me gain a measure of control of my emotions.

"I'm usually a lot tougher," I sobbed.

"I hope so," she said, "because usually so am I." Her voice softened. I detected more playfulness than aggravation. "The next time you won't get off so lightly."

"I have clothing for you," my Mistress said, "but for now I want you naked."

My shirt, shoes, pants, socks and shorts were lying in a pile on the floor near me.

"Now up, boy," she said, tossing me a fine linen pillow case. "Put your clothes in here. I will keep them for you."

I rose, exposed and fully extended, and did as she requested. Before I placed my pants in the pillow case, I removed my wallet.

"I will keep that for you, too," she said.

"But —"

"While you are in my service, you are not allowed money of your own. I will decide what your needs are and provide them for you."

"But my driver's license —"

"Obey the law and you will not need to show it. Anyway, if you drive, it will be in one of my vehicles. The plates are personalized, known to the local police, whom I support generously. Or do you think I will steal from you?"

I tossed the wallet in and she took it from me.

"Come!" she turned and walked.

I followed behind her. She led me to the mud room.

"You will find polish and rags in that cabinet," she said. "Clean and shine these boots."

She walked off and left me to the task. I took one of the shoes in hand and began wiping the caked dirt and dried grass clippings from it. I smelled inside. Even the sweat of her feet was voluptuous. I was tempted to release my lust, but, as I understood my Mistress, she might call at any time and I was to be ardent. I could not risk disappointing her.

An hour later she came to check on me.

"Not finished yet? You're slow. When you do finish, bring the boots to my room. That's up the stairs, left, and to the end of the hall."

The tension I felt was enormous. Eager to see her again, I worked as fast as I could. But my bruised shoulder made quick movement painful. I looked in the mirror. She left a bright red and blue discoloration several inched in diameter.

It was nearly six when I finished. I could see my face in every heel and toe. As I carried the boots upstairs, my blood pounded. The expectation of being with her in her bedroom was so intense I thought I might faint. Trembling but standing tall, I knocked on her door.

"Come in."

A large portrait of Madam and her horse hung over the fireplace and dominated the luxurious bedroom. The bed, set in a cozy nook of sponge-painted pink walls, was a four-poster with a canopy and an upholstered headboard. Draped in gauzy silk and covered with lace-edged linens, cashmere blankets and fur throws, it was a proper sleeping place for the embodiment of the Goddess. She was lounging on a chaise in a dressing gown. She had a fashion magazine on her lap. She looked at me and I was captivated by her gaze. She seemed a Divine Being who could penetrate me and read my thoughts and feelings. I remembered her order that I was not to look directly at her. I lowered my eyes. Her calves were long and smooth, her feet were slender and delicate, and her toenails shined with red enamel.

"Look at you!" she said, and laughed with a teasing lilt. "Back from boot camp, eh? Let me show you where to put them."

She was about to rise from the chaise when the telephone rang. She sank back down, looked at me and held up a finger. I understood that I was to wait.

"Oh hello, Peter, I was just thinking of you, darling."

She motioned me to come closer to her. While she spoke to Peter, she toyed with me. The self-satisfied smirk on her face said she enjoyed her own wickedness as much as she enjoyed fondling me.

"Yes, we're invited to dinner at Rene's. Pick me up at eight? . . .Oh, you miss me, do you? Well, I can't wait to see you, darling . . ."

I stood there submissively at attention and let her trifle as she would.

" . . .Super, darling. Bye, now!"

When she finished her conversation she looked up at me.

"You silly boy! Because you're so sweet, you have the privilege of serving as my valet. Isn't that exciting?"

I was elated.

She said, "When I ask for an article of clothing or an accessory, I want you to know which I mean and where you can find it."

She showed me to her closets, a trio of connected chambers, each twice the size of the room I had at the boarding house. In the first room there were racks of casual suits. I saw nubby wools, fine linens, clinging silks, flowing soft cottons and luxurious microfibers. I noticed that many of her skirts, pants and jackets, while plain without, had decorative motifs and sensual fabrics in the linings, as if she did not want to share her costly extravagances with anyone. She had hundreds of blouses, tank tops and polo shirts. She showed me several antique cedar chests full of soft wool sweaters.

In the second room I saw drawers of swimwear and racks of tennis dresses. There was a large wardrobe of riding jackets and pants and another of robes, kimonos and bed jackets. She kept her undergarments in a delicately carved bureau. She gave me the complete tour of her lace: brassieres, briefs, tap pants, camisoles, leotards, panties, teddies, slips and loungewear. I could barely contain myself. A separate, similar cabinet held her hosiery, everything from woolen leg warmers to silk stockings, panty hose to tennis socks. There were tights and cat suits made of stretchy synthetic materials that fit close to her body.

The last room was devoted entirely to leather. There were skirts, jackets, footwear, bags, belts and three fine French saddles. She showed me a multi-tiered rack that ran the length of the wall. It held over two hundred pairs of shoes. I found room for her boots.

The overall impression I got was that my Mistress

dressed conservatively, with casual elegance, but had an eye — and certainly the figure — for occasional flamboyance.

She told me that it was my responsibility to see that every item of her clothing was hanging properly or folded neatly. The shining of her shoes and the handwashing of her stockings, underwear and other intimate apparel were also my domain. I told her that I was honored being allowed in this inner sanctum and to touch her things after she had worn them was a happiness more than I could describe. I promised I would do my best to see that everything would be just the way she liked it.

She laughed, reached down and, with a mischievous smile, petted me with her slender, soft palm. "I better not catch you sniffing my panties and playing with yourself," she said.

I panted like a dog. I wanted more. But she moved away. It was a game. She seemed very satisfied with herself. She was a wicked teaser.

There was another door behind her shoe closet. It had a bolt on the outside and a key in the lock.

"Here are your quarters," she said as she slid back the bolt and turned the key.

My room was a small bare cell with no window. On the floor in the far left corner was a narrow sleeping pallet. At the foot of the pallet was a low table with a gooseneck lamp. On the other side of the room was a toilet and a small wash tub. On the lip of the tub were bars of soap, several containers of bath oils and skin lotions.

"I hope I don't have to talk to you about personal hygiene," she said. "You're to be squeaky clean, morning, noon and night."

There was another door on the far wall. She showed me that it led to the main hall on the second floor.

"You can come or go through here without disturbing me," she said.

I noticed that there was a lock and a bolt on the outside of this door, too. It was possible for her to lock me in my room, yet I had no way to protect my own privacy.

"Ummmm," she groaned. "I suddenly feel out of sorts." She stretched and stroked her neck. "I'm getting my period," she announced in a husky voice that bristled with soreness. "I think I'll take a bath."

She ordered me to bring champagne. I took a while locating the vintage she asked for, the ice bucket and glass. By the time I arrived in her bath, the air was steamy and fragrant with bath oils. She was lying back in the tub with her eyes half-closed, soaking in a hot soapy meringue, listening to a disc of Mozart piano concerti. Through the bubbles I could see her nipples. They were large and turned up. Without looking at me, she reached out. I filled a crystal flute with champagne and handed it to her. She sipped and murmured, "Stay and serve."

We passed a half-hour thus. She only seemed to notice me if I was late filling her glass. I understood I shouldn't stare, but I couldn't keep my eyes off her. Her aches and pains relieved, her face became serene and more lovely. She was so beautiful it hurt.

A rapid flutter of excitement passed through me when she rose from the suds and rinsed herself in the shower. I saw the triangular puff of soft hair that crowned her queen-piece.

"Get in the tub," she said, wrapping herself in a terry cloth bath robe.

Dipping into water which contained her womanly secretions was intoxicating. I immersed myself and ladled water on my head. I felt that being baptized in her blood put me on the road to heaven.

When I got out of the tub, she rubbed against me. I quivered in her arms. Then she kissed me and whispered that she loved me.

27

I was overjoyed, charged with a greater happiness than I had ever known.

"And I love you," I whispered back and tried to kiss her again.

But she turned a cold cheek.

"Of course, you do," she said with a brisk indifference that deflated me.

She had me fetch different ensembles. I laid out six possibilities on her bed before she decided on basic black: a lace bra and panties, a full skirt, a long-sleeved top which showed her fine bustline and high-heels. She chose a gold chain-belt. She gave me a few playful smacks with the buckle and told me to imagine the sting of a full flailing.

When she was ready to go out, my Mistress was every bit a Lady. I could not decide whether she was more breathtaking unclothed or clothed.

"Before you go to bed," she said, "you are to clean the kitchen. I'm sure you can find something to eat. Then tidy up my room, turn down my bed covers, and be in your room by ten. I don't want to find you idling around the house when I come home. If I need help getting ready for bed, I'll call you. And, remember, you must not play with yourself! If you're a bad boy, I'll know! I know everything about you. And I'm going to examine you, if not later tonight then tomorrow. You better be stiffer than this." She flicked her fingers against my eager flesh.

I nodded.

"I won't have a servant who is not master of himself."

I was weak with desire. The bruise on my shoulder burned as I washed the dishes, scrubbed the range and wiped the counters. I ate cold chicken and salad. Afterwards I went upstairs and put back the clothing my Mistress decided against. I found the panties she had worn that day on the floor and sniffed at the crotch. It might as well have been cocaine. The sharp carnal note of her insides and her heavy, spicy perfume drove me mad with need. She was under my skin. She was on my mind, watching me. At the same time, I wondered if she was thinking about me at all. I was tempted to ejaculate, but I caught myself. I wanted to be all for her.

I lay down on my pallet and fell into a light sleep. I woke just after midnight when I heard her come in. My senses were elevated and I was harder than ever. I sat up, praying she would call me. I heard footsteps on the stairs, then voices, hers and a man's. My heart sank. She was taking someone else to bed. Peter. I felt a sudden, biting rage. I buried my head in the pillow. Unable to control myself any longer and consumed by thoughts of her sweet flesh, I came on my bed.

"Boy!"

I heard her voice in my dream. She wanted me. I jumped up. It was seven-thirty in the morning. I quickly washed and combed my hair. Still without clothing, I made my way through her closets and knocked softly on her bedroom door.

"Enter!"

I found her lying in bed, her hair dishevelled, her silk nightshirt open. The man was gone. I was thankful for that. Seeing her naked breasts and smelling the cloying, morning-after musk of her lair, I became stiff and feverish with excitement all over again. When I presented myself to her, I did not think she could tell I violated her order to contain myself.

She groaned and rubbed her eyes. She said she had too much to drink the night before and had a devilish headache. She directed me to her medicine cabinet where I would find aspirin.

I brought the bottle and glass of water and, noticing it was now seven forty-five, went to make her coffee. Still learning my way around the kitchen, I was not back until five minutes past eight. My Mistress was very irritated.

"You will bring my coffee at *eight* every morning. After today, you will receive a lash for every minute I have to wait."

She took a sip of the coffee and said it was too weak. I went back and made another pot. This, too, she sent back, saying it was still too weak. When I brought the third pot she sipped it and said it was too strong.

"What kind of houseservant makes such bad coffee?"

I apologized and offered to try again.

"Quiet!" she said. "I don't know what I'm going to do with you! You've wasted a half-hour of my time! Get out of my sight! Wait in the hall until I call you."

For a half-hour I stood outside her bedroom. I prayed to the Goddess she was not going to terminate the try-out.

"Here, boy." When my Mistress called, my heart tore between fear and longing.

Her hair was combed, her night-shirt buttoned. She had a pad of paper on her lap and was writing. Her annoyance about the coffee had apparently passed. She asked me to put away the clothing she had worn to dinner.

When she finished writing she ordered me to fetch her robe and slippers. I held the robe open for her. When she slid out of bed to put it on, I once again saw the wispy hair that grew over the zenith of her power.

I went to my knees to help her with her slippers. There was a short white string hanging from her lower lips.

She told me she had a great many friends who summered in the area and who stayed on through the fall foliage before leaving for their homes in Florida or the islands. As a consequence, there were social invitations through the end of October.

"Today I'm having two friends over for lunch, Lilith Harrod and Rene Eblis. I'll want you to serve a green salad, some crusty French bread and grilled salmon steaks. Do you think you can handle that?"

"I think so, Madam."

"Good," she said. "Lunch will be at one o'clock sharp, on the patio."

She handed me the paper. It was a list of errands.

"As much as I would like to, I can't send you out naked."

At that moment a truck came up the drive. A delivery man left several packages on the porch by the kitchen door. When she sent me to retrieve them for her, I saw they bore the labels of Manhattan's most expensive men's shops.

The first box she opened contained three pairs of white cotton shorts. She gave me a pair to try on. The cotton was the most luxurious imaginable. The fit was snug. Both stretchy and clinging, the garment hugged me front and back. Having been naked for almost eighteen hours, my skin was sensitive to the pressure of the material. She put her hand up my leg, into the shorts, and felt. "Enough room in there for you, big boy?"

I swelled with the compliment. But even though I was mad with desire, my Mistress still showed no sign of finishing what she had started yesterday during my interview. She nonchalantly opened the next package. It contained several pairs of sheer black silk hose. Another package contained white linen shirts. Another had several pairs of black silk trousers. Another had a pair of black loafers. There was also a black silk windbreaker which I would need when the weather got cooler.

Everything fit perfectly. She guessed my exact sizes. The idea that she thought about me made my heart beat with love and wonder.

In the last box, there was a short-brimmed groom's cap. Embossed with the insignia of Lavender Hill Farm, it expressed *underling*. I cringed as I put it on. It made me feel three inches shorter.

She stood back, looked me over and laughed. "Now you look like a proper-looking young manservant. People may talk, but that is all the better. I want them to see that you work for me and I want you to be aware of it, too."

She pulled me by the collar and in front of the mirror. I saw a dandy monkey looking back at me. She pulled out her bloodstained tampon and waved it in front of me, holding it by the string. "It looks as if I have a wounded white mouse by the tail." She laughed. She was fooling.

And what a fool she was making of me! Still, if this mean amusement was what she wanted, I was thrilled to be able to provide it for her.

"In my service, when you are out of the house, you must wear this livery. Since you are only on trial here, you better keep your room in the boarding house. You will need a place to go should I dismiss you. How much is your rent?"

"Sixty dollars a week," I told her. She went into her purse and came back with four crisp hundreds.

"This is for six weeks. Bring me the change."

I took the money and praised her for her fairness.

She gave no acknowledgement of my appreciation. "I don't want you bringing anything of yours into my house."

I pled for my notebook.

"Of course," she relented. "You may keep what pens and paper you need in your room. I won't have a typewriter. The noise is bothersome."

I thanked her for her indulgence.

Today she had jumping practice at the stables at ten. I was to wait while she bathed and dressed. Before I could leave on my round of errands, she wanted me to straighten her room, make her bed and clean her bath.

On her way out, she gave me a sharp blow on the back of my legs with her crop.

"That is for playing with what is now mine," she said.

"You know I ejaculated?"

"I know everything!" she said. "Don't think you can fool me. There is nothing you can hide from me. You are a bad boy, wanton. You revel in your own debasement, don't you?"

"Yes, Madam."

"That's shameful."

"Yes, Madam."

"You're lucky you have me to punish you for your waywardness and set you on the right path. But I cannot have you up to snuff in six weeks without your effort. If you want this position, you must make a decision to obey my rules."

"Yes, Madam."

It was nearly eleven o'clock when I finally made it out of the house. It was going to be difficult to do all the errands and still have lunch ready at one. She wanted me to feel pressure. There was a van in the garage that I was to use. As I drove the lumbering beast, I longed for her. Would she tease me to death? What would she do if lunch was late or not up to her standards?

First I went to the boarding house. The uniform made me feel self-conscious. That was its purpose. Mrs Gooden was disappointed in me.

"Won't see your dreams come true working for the likes of that witch," she predicted with clipped Yankee candor. "Knew Burke Ketchener when she was a little girl. Wasn't worth much then, worth less now."

She was delighted when I paid for my room six weeks in advance.

33

I had pick-ups at the grocery store, the liquor store, the dry cleaners, the riding shop, the dress shop, the shoe store and the drug store. I wondered what medication my Mistress took. The bag the druggist gave me was stapled shut. I dared not pry.

After getting the fish and putting gas in the van, I made my way back to Lavender Hill. Slowed down by construction along Twin Ponds Highway, I squirmed nervously. Although I had not wasted a minute, I found myself short of time. I couldn't bear the thought of being late and disappointing my Mistress.

When I got to the house it was just before noon. My Mistress was still out. I put the things I collected in the appropriate places and began to prepare lunch.

Spurred by fear of displeasing her, by a quarter to one I had the table set, the bread sliced, the wine chilled, the fish marinated, the grill hot and the salad ready to be dressed. My Mistress arrived. Very energetic after her ride, she paced to and fro, casting her demanding eyes over everything I had done. She reprimanded me for my table setting. I was rearranging the forks and the flowers when I heard the cars pull up.

A few moments later two women appeared on the patio. I understood that as a servant, when there was company, I was not supposed to stare. My place was to be unobtrusive, like a piece of the decor, yet attentive, making sure guests had whatever they needed. When the women entered, curiosity got the better of me. I cast a furtive eye over them.

One was tall, fit and sun-tanned and wore glasses. She was older than my Mistress. Her face was somewhat worn and there was dissipation in her eyes, but she was still very handsome. Her dark hair had a streak of gray and was tied in a French twist. She was wearing heels, pleated silk shorts, knee-length, and a jacket.

"Lilith, darling!" My Mistress kissed the older women first. This was Mrs Harrod.

"Burke, darling."

The other, Mrs Eblis, was younger. She was medium height, blonde, large-breasted, and was dressed casually in loafers, a white cotton blouse and skin-tight stretch pants.

"Rene, darling!" My Mistress kissed her.

"Burke, darling."

"And what's this?" said Mrs Harrod, as I brought out a tray with three glasses of white wine. "Have you gotten a new toy?"

"Perhaps," said my Mistress. "It depends on how he behaves himself.'

Mrs Harrod took her wine from the tray and walked around me. She was having a look at my backside.

They all laughed. I, apparently, was the joke.

I was not the center of attention for more than a few seconds however. "We're both dying to know all about last night," Mrs Harrod said to my Mistress. "How was Peter?"

My Mistress made a lustful snicker and the other two cackled. Peter, too, was a joke.

The three sat down. I served the food and poured more wine.

When my Mistress began to tell about her evening with Peter, the pangs of jealousy made me retreat into the kitchen to clean up.

"Where are you, boy?" my Mistress called. "We'll have more lemon slices."

As I brought out the lemon, I could not shut my ears. "Peter has a long tongue," my Mistress was saying, "but not very much in his pants."

She bragged how she got him worked up and then sent him home.

"So, Burke darling, what are you up to with this boy?" asked Mrs Eblis.

My Mistress smoothed her hair and gave a nasty chuckle.

"I hope you're not going to be too hard on him, darling," Mrs Harrod laughed. "Boys like this have fragile hearts."

Mrs Eblis looked at me with an arrogant smirk. "He's just the sort a real woman loves to break."

"Now, don't frighten the poor thing, darlings," said my Mistress. "He doesn't seem as if he's made of very stern stuff. Hurry, stupid boy, more wine. And bring my slippers. These boots are pinching my feet."

The three of them laughed as I poured the wine and went upstairs to fetch my Mistress's slippers. I was stung, feeling that I would explode from chagrin, and yet my Mistress's air of prerogative pushed me to a passion beyond any I had ever known. By the time I returned to the patio, my excitement was plainly visible. I tried to conceal my embarrassment behind the slippers.

I went to my knees beside my Mistress and began to unlace her left boot. To sport with me, she kept moving her foot, making my task impossible. Her friends laughed at my distress and both made remarks about the bulge in my pants. I was thoroughly flustered and yet my urgency continued to mount. My Mistress pressed her boot toe between my thighs and gave me a menacing nudge. The power of her touch was so intense I was afraid I might wet my pants. I prayed to the Goddess for strength. Fortunately, Mrs Harrod went on gossiping about a woman named Thalia Thorndyke. My Mistress, interested in what tidbit was being proffered, withdrew her foot and allowed me to exchange the boots for the slippers.

Lunch seemed very jolly. The women drank and laughed until three when there was a round of kisses and "Bye, darlings."

I was at the kitchen sink washing the glasses and

watching Mrs Harrod and Mrs Eblis through the window as they drove off when I felt a firm tap on my back.

"Madam!" I said, turning.

My Mistress had her crop.

"I hope everything was satisfactory."

"Hardly!" she said in her harsh whisper. She grabbed me by the hair and told me that the service was slow, the fish overdone, and the way I allowed my erection to show in front of her guests was an outrage.

"Drop your pants and bend over!"

I did not try to fight her. I did as she asked and let her give me a sharp blow across the buttocks. The pain radiated up my back and down my legs. I gasped and she gave me another blow. I cried and begged her forgiveness. I promised that my intention was to please her and that such lapses would never happen again. "They had better not," she muttered roughly and hit me again. It hurt so much I sunk to my knees and crawled under the antique maple side table.

She came after me.

"Your shirt had a spot on it."

She hit the edge of the table as hard as she could. The crack was deafening. The table tilted. Splinters flew. I shook in terror of what such a blow would do to my tender flesh.

"There was too much oil in the salad."

Crack! She hit the table again.

"You were too slow taking away the plates."

Crack!

"You were lax about pouring the wine."

Crack!

"The coffee was too strong."

Crack!

With each crack on the table I felt myself get smaller. My tears choked my apologies. Even so, my passion was whipped up.

She ordered me out of my hiding place.

Seething with emotion, I obeyed.

"Bend over the table!"

I saw the series of marks she had made in the wood and recoiled.

"Now! Or you'll make things worse for yourself."

I did as I was told.

"So far this has been for your education," she laughed. "But I don't need sufficient reason to punish you other than I feel like doing so."

She hit me.

"That was for my pleasure. When it's your fault it's your fault; when it's not your fault you get double. Those new boots hurt my feet." She gave me another blow. "And I found the conversation at lunch tedious. I sometimes think my so-called friends talk about me behind my back." She hit me twice more. "I can't very well punish them, so I punish you. It makes *me* feel better. Do you think that's fair?"

The queen must be right, doubly so when she is wrong.

"Yes, yes, Madam, very fair."

"You will stay in this position until I tell you to move."

She left the kitchen. After a half-hour she returned. Not only was I passionately in love, I was scared stiff, anticipating what she might do. My terror taught me of the importance of pleasing her and the hopelessness of the task. But she stroked my head gently.

"I did not really mean to hurt you, but I have to think of myself, don't I? You are my property. How are you going to learn unless you fear me?"

Her soft touch brought me immense happiness. It dispelled all my fear of her. She played with my erection and when I shivered on the verge of a climax, she yawned.

"I'm going upstairs for a nap," she said. "As for you, pull up your pants and finish cleaning up."

When I inspected my injuries in the mirror, I was surprised to see only the slightest discolorations where the crop had hit me. The bruise on my shoulder, however, now several days old, showed no sign of healing.

As I scoured the sink, I thought I would explode. I prayed fervently to the Goddess to intercede and prompt my Mistress to take pity on me.

"Boy!" I heard my Mistress call from upstairs.

"Yes, Madam?"

"I want you here."

I was trembling as I walked up the stairs, down the hall and into her bedroom. I fell to my knees and told her I was her slave and would do anything she asked.

She sat on the edge of the chaise and asked me to remove her slippers. I savored every moment of my service. When I saw her feet, smooth and dainty, I became so aroused I couldn't stop myself from bending forward and kissing her toes.

She gave a short but solid kick and hit my lip. "I didn't ask for that slobbering. Take off your clothing, everything. Be quick about it."

She stood and paced impatiently as I undressed. When I was naked she grabbed me firmly by the shoulder and pushed me face-down on the bed. The pillows had her sultry smell. Without a moment's hesitation she fell on top of me. I felt paralyzed under her. There was so much sensation: her warm lips at my ear, her arms on my shoulders, her breasts against my back, the zipper of her riding britches rubbing between my buttocks. The expert way she rode me expressed her intention to reduce me to a thing that existed for her pleasure.

"Are you *really* mine? Do I *fully* own you?" she asked.

I nodded my head and gasped, "Yes, Madam, I'm fully yours."

"And are you *completely* at my mercy?"

"Yes, Madam, completely."

She reached around my stomach and gently stroked her mouse. "And do you find me merciful?"

"Yes, Madam."

She began to squeeze hard. She frightened me.

"No more," I begged her.

"I do as I wish," she squeezed harder.

She had a spasm of pleasure and relaxed her grip.

For all my discomfort, I was on the point of ejaculation, but I caught myself. I was proud of myself for remaining continent.

She lay still for a moment, then got up.

"Roll over, boy," she said. She saw my prick was harder and redder, readier than ever.

"Stay!" she commanded as she went to the bathroom.

I dared not move.

She came back changed into a luxurious robe, quilted satin and fur. Her face, in the flush of excitement, looked so lovely I could not take my eyes from her. She climbed on the bed and she slapped me, pushing my head to one side. "How dare you look directly at your Mistress!"

She straddled my thighs so the mouse seemed to protrude from her. She held it with a deliberateness that suggested a sacred ritual and brushed its sensitive under-belly with the fur hem of her sleeve. The tickling sensation was so overpowering I begged her to allow me release. She smiled, grabbed me by the throat, and growled softly, "You come when I say!"

Then she pulled me inside her and began to move, telling me over and over that I belonged to her.

"I do, Madam! I am yours! I am you!" I moaned and held her tighter. Even though she was smaller than I, I felt engulfed, totally absorbed, in her warm smooth body.

She looked at her breasts and began to touch them. She was as madly in love with herself as I was. The sight, the smell and the warm feel of her were too much for both of us. She began to tremble with pleasure.

"Now!" she commanded.

Caught in her tender trap, her mouse gave up its ghost.

The boundaries between us melted. When I came inside of her, she came inside of me and swallowed me body and soul. I felt complete; at the same time, I felt that I no longer existed. I was hers entirely, and yet not a molecule of her was mine. There was only her, Madam.

After the roar of orgasm, I felt calm. I was lulled by her warm flesh. Half-dozing, I leaned tenderly toward her and told her how beautiful she was and that I felt the greatest joy and privilege being one with her.

She did not look my way or acknowledge that I had spoken. She slid off me, took a cigarette from the pack on the table and held it, waiting for me to light it. I obliged her. She inhaled deeply and blew a long plume of smoke in my face. She gave me a hard, unfeeling look and moved her eyes toward the door. Then she picked up a novel which was on her bedside table, opened to her place and began reading.

I was wounded by the dismissal. As I closed the door behind me, the wholeness I felt evaporated. There seemed to be more distance between us than ever. She had taken something from me. Now she was twice the woman and I was half the man. Henceforth, I would need her to be whole.

She remained in her quarters for the remainder of the day. A new tension mounted within me. I could not get the thought of how she looked, felt and smelled out of my mind. In the heat of the moment, she seemed to enjoy what we did immensely. Yet now I had a feeling that I had done something wrong. But what was it? Maybe I was too forward afterwards; maybe I did not say enough how beautiful she was; maybe I was personally offensive to her in some way. I thought of a thousand "maybes" but I knew nothing for sure.

I was split in two. The man in me wanted to walk out on her. But beauty had the upper hand on the beast. The animal in me was more beguiled than ever.

The following morning when I brought my Mistress her coffee, I knocked softly but there was no answer. The door was ajar. I peeked and saw she was fast asleep, half out of the bed covers. Unsure of whether to come back later or to comply with her standing request for coffee at eight, I looked at her breasts and thighs and my heart fluttered. I wished her a good morning, placed the coffee beside her and drew back the curtains.

She opened her eyes, shook her head, yawned, stretched and sat up in bed. I asked if there was anything she needed, but, to my disappointment, she sunk back into her pillows. Without saying a word or even looking at me, she took a sip of coffee.

I was watering the geraniums on the porch when she left for the stables. She looked perfect. I said good day. She did not reply. I asked her if there was anything I might do for her, but she breezed by me as if I didn't exist.

Her total disregard for me was a worse torture than her teasing. Her acknowledgement of me was everything. Without it, I was nothing.

I took it upon myself to change the linens on her bed and scrub her tub, shower, sink, toilet and bidet. The kitchen floor looked as if it had been not been cleaned in a while. I got down on my knees and washed and polished it until it sparkled. I was just finishing when she came back from her ride.

Without a word, she went about making herself a cup of coffee. She did not seem to notice that the floor had been cleaned. She had mud and sand on her boots. As she paced back and forth impatiently, waiting for the coffee to be ready, the floor that I had so carefully cleaned and shined was scraped and soiled. I dared not draw it to her attention. Mug in hand, she walked by me without a look or a nod and disappeared upstairs. It took me another hour to wipe up the dirt and buff the scuff marks.

I was washing the floor in the mud room when she reappeared. She was dressed softly, in a wool sweater and a pleated skirt. I did not even try to speak to her. I could tell by the look in her eye that she would ignore me. She left the house, got in her car and sped off to a luncheon date.

There was left-over bread and fish in the refrigerator. I fixed myself a sandwich, but I was too upset to eat it. I hungered for my Mistress's delicious body. Hoping to gain her approval, I spent the rest of the afternoon cleaning.

At four o'clock I was sweeping the garage when I saw my Mistress coming up the drive. She drove into the garage as if she didn't see me. She would have run me over had I not quickly stepped aside. Behind her was another car, a convertible, driven by a fair-skinned man with a pink cashmere sweater draped over his back. The sleeves were tied in a knot under his chin. This, I guessed, was Peter. What did she see in him? My rival looked like a smug sissy to me.

She led him right past me into the house. I was too distraught to continue my sweeping. I sat on the patio as darkness fell, trying to suppress the passion I felt. Now that I had been with her, being without her was infinitely more painful. Imagining another man in my place was a hellish torment.

Finally Peter returned to his car and departed. I went back into the house. My Mistress was dressed for dinner and on her way out. She seemed in a hurry. I broke down crying, asking her what I had done to deserve such cold treatment. She walked by me without even looking at me.

I went to my quarters. I thought how utterly I had been spurned and I began to cry. I pounded my head with my fists to stop the pain that raged within me. I got up and went into her bath. I found her panties in the hamper. Sniffing her perfume, her piss and her sweat, I lost control of myself.

The following morning, I woke before dawn. In the quiet, in the darkness, I worried. Now that my Mistress had had me, would she dismiss me? Or would she keep me, knowing I loved her, and never let me touch her again? At least if she would speak to me . . .

I turned to my notebook and read what I had written. I felt detached from the characters in my novel. I prayed to the Muse. I vowed to accept my circumstances whatever they were for the sake of my art.

Suddenly I felt obliged to put my novel aside. I turned a new leaf and began to record my own experiences. The words came effortlessly. I celebrated the extremes of joy and pain, the absurdity and the paradox of the love I felt. Describing the way she took me, I became so feverishly excited I nearly wet the paper, but I resisted and by seven-thirty I had spilled several pages of text.

When I brought my Mistress her coffee, I felt peaceful, refreshed and resigned to her will. I found her awake, reading a book of essays by Donald Guermantes. Guermantes was an academic Marxist with a critical view of America's popular culture. The rage in universities and trendy intellectual circles, he envisioned a sexless, compulsory *esprit de corps* among men and women. I thought of him as Cotton Mather in blue jeans.

I wished my Mistress good morning. I told her she

looked beautiful. She did not reply or even look from her book. I carried on silently and efficiently, setting the tray down and serving her. She dismissed me with a wave of her hand.

Later, my Mistress came down dressed in her most serious riding costume: a red hunting jacket with gold buttons, braid and epaulets. She did not give me a list of chores but I kept busy. She did not return until late in the afternoon. I was bringing clean towels to her bath. Without warning she shoved me against the wall.

"You're not a man," she growled, "you're a pussy." These, the first words she had said to me in two days, were a beautiful sound.

She dragged me by the hair to her bed, pushed me on my belly, pulled down my pants, and pressed the handle of her crop against my anus.

As much as it hurt, I was excited by the attack. My attempt to fight back was feeble, just enough to add some satisfaction to her conquest. She pushed in roughly. I cried in pain as she writhed in the throes of a villainess's pleasure.

When she withdrew her instrument, a few drops of blood issued from a tear in my delicate tissue.

The sight of it infuriated her.

"How dare you stain your Mistress's linens! Do you have any idea what sheets like these cost? It's a privilege that I let you on them."

I apologized, but she forced the crop in me again, this time breaking my cherry wide open.

"Let it bleed, bitch-boy," she snarled. "Now that my sheet is ruined, it doesn't matter."

She had her way but would not permit me an ejaculation. As I changed the sheets on her bed, she showered. She had me attend her as she dressed and packed an overnight bag. She was going to New York City with Peter for the evening.

Before she left she informed me that tomorrow was her day to entertain the ladies of the Norbury Riding Club.

"Lunch will be for thirteen, and it had better be perfect."

She looked at me with a reproachful, edgy glare that promised severe consequences if I should disappoint her. I felt aroused by her irritability. She gave me a menu which included Cornish hens, rice pilaf and salad.

I promised her I would take care of everything with the eye to excellence she demanded. I felt my heart rip in two when she left. I sought refuge in my writing. Late to bed and early to rise, I worked most of the night, pouring my thoughts and feelings onto the page.

When I returned with the groceries for lunch it was ten-thirty. My Mistress had come back from New York and was on the telephone in the parlor, talking to a friend in Europe, arranging a trip she was planning in November. She made some other calls and then came into the kitchen and looked over my shoulder. I was nervous enough, cooking for thirteen. But she made me more so. Nevertheless, I got the game hens in the oven and prepared the pilaf and salad. I longed for her approval and was proud of myself that at least I received no reprimand.

At one o'clock I had the dining room table set. The cars came up the drive. There was Whitney Wette, Mrs Singleton-Steiner, Mrs Rosen, Miss Trilling and a Beverly Hills heiress, a devastating beauty in a revealing sun dress named Lisa Cummings. Madame Bayard and Mrs Oistereich, senior members of the club, both had malevolent sneers etched in their once pretty faces. These old schoolgirls gave me the impression they were merciless slave drivers. There was a heavy-set woman named Mrs Morrisey, a good-looking woman in a feathered cap named Mrs Treadways and a horse-faced one, extremely rich, named Layne Morgan. Mrs Eblis and Mrs Harrod arrived last, together. I could see that they, along with my Mistress, were the leaders of this rat pack of spoiled women.

The coven drank wine and chatted furiously. Ms Wette was on the board of Amnesty International and a generous supporter of the Red Cross and the American Civil Liberties Union. I heard her tell Mrs Treadways how unhappy she was with her gardener. Although Miguel worked for a third of what Norbury's native sons charged, Ms Wette did not think he was worth it. Mrs Treadways was sympathetic to Ms Wette's problem. Her new Mexican gardener had butchered her favorite azalea.

Mrs Morrisey told Mrs Rosen about her recent trip to China. She praised that nation for the strides it was making for the welfare of its people. She wished the United States would take a lesson. There was a general disapproving murmur when the ladies heard the name of their country mentioned.

"The paltry sums our government spends on the arts," sneered Mrs Trilling, "makes us the laughingstock of Europe."

Mrs Morrisey and Ms Morgan talked about horses, saddles and riding gear. Mrs Harrod was a vicious gossip. As she picked at her hen, she gloated over a story about someone named Adele who was going through a mean divorce. Mrs Harrod seemed to stir everyone else to new heights in nastiness. They had their airs of taste and fine breeding, but they were an uncouth, insensitive lot. They slurred friends who were not present. They ridiculed the men in their lives. Those who had husbands spoke derisively of them. Like my Mistress, they all had affairs with men of their social class, whom they found inadequate. They snickered about the fun they had making service-class men feel like dirt. These witches spoke frankly of carnal acts and private parts. They related their sexual adventures with the same nonchalance that they described shopping for shoes.

My Mistress was discussing the differences between European and American lovers with Madame Bayard. She had her back turned to me as I filled Miss Cumming's glass with wine. I cast a furtive, longing glance down Miss Cummings's dress. I imagined my little trespass went unobserved, but when I looked up, I saw my Mistress, telepathic, had turned. She was glaring at me.

Mrs Treadways was looking at me too. She held up her glass for me to fill.

"Wherever did you find this darling boy?" she said to my Mistress as I poured. "If you ever have a notion to sell him, you must let me know. I'd love to snatch him from you."

Before dessert my Mistress rose and gave a little speech. She welcomed the ladies and reminded them that she was the chairperson for the local chapter of the Committee to Elect Fay Goodman. Goodman, a vanity candidate for Governor, quite wealthy, was a strident feminist who preached a paternalistic dogma about the evils of sexual harassment and the need for more social programs. She once advocated the censorship of rock and roll. The ladies all dug into their hand-made Italian leather handbags for their checkbooks.

All present congratulated themselves on their magnanimity, tolerance and open-mindedness. I thanked the Goddess that Ms Goodman had little chance of being elected.

Like my Mistress, these ladies lived in a fantasy world. They grew up in affluent households where they were pampered, overprotected and no doubt neglected by wealthy, emotionally-repressed parents. Their espousal of welfare-state programs reflected their expectations of a safe world, tamed by money. Their refusal to acknowledge a woman's responsibility for her sex's role in the mating dance made them eager to see laws enacted preventing boys from being boys.

Lunch was over at three. When the ladies left, I began to clean up. I thought everything was as my Mistress ordered, but she came into the kitchen, swinging her crop, seething with anger. She told me that I was completely worthless, a total embarrassment to her. Everyone had seen me ogling Miss Cummings.

She ordered me to drop my pants and drawers and stand, bent forward, over the kitchen table. I pleaded with her to have mercy.

"Do as I say, you little sneak, or you will make things worse for yourself."

I did as she commanded. My bare bottom quivered in fear.

Again, my Mistress left for the evening. I never heard her return.

I woke the next morning at the crack of dawn with the prayer to the Goddess on my lips. I checked if my Mistress's car was parked in the drive. It was not. I spent the day with my notebook. Recounting my lovesickness always seemed to calm me down. Evening came and she still was not back. I retired. Around midnight I heard her come in. She was alone. I was glad for that. I looked forward to the morning when I would see her. I woke early and wrote. Then I went down to make her coffee. I found a note taped to the pot.

> Will be sleeping late.
> Bring coffee at ten.

The delay was disappointing. I went back to my room and struggled with my impulse to ejaculate. I did not succumb.

I stood up hard and tall as I served my Mistress her coffee. She expected this in her presence and was usually nonchalant about it. Today, she became quite flirtatious. She complimented me on my erection. She motioned me to lie next to her on the bed. The phone rang. It was Peter. While she cooed to him, she put her hands into my shorts and played with me. I thrilled to her touch and made myself completely available.

She made plans to see Peter later and ended the conversation. She pressed against me and shuddered with pleasure. "I'm spoiling you by keeping you in the house, boy," she said. She presented me with a package that contained khaki shorts and a sweat shirt, work gloves and work boots.

Dressed in this gardener's uniform, I followed her across the south lawn, past the extensive rose garden and trellises of rare honeysuckle and clematis, down a gradual slope.

"I'm a fanatic about my garden," my Mistress boasted. She lectured me for ten minutes about the economy of Mother Nature, how she lets nothing go to waste.

From what I had seen so far, Burke Ketchener was more apt to squander than she was to conserve. Although her sermon on ecology rang hollow, I said, "Yes, Madam," to her on every point.

The garden shed was behind a tall hedgerow. Next to it, toward the horse barns, sat three huge piles of horse manure in various stages of decay. The stable boys collected it and brought it there. She ordered me to spread the composted pile on the roses and the several flower beds around the house. Then I was to turn over the other two piles and move them to make room for more. As the garden paths were too narrow to allow a tractor, I would have to use a handcart to push the loads up the incline and distribute them.

It was hard labor designed to keep me strong and aware of my place. She took a bamboo garden stake from the shed and watched me as I shovelled the first load into the cart. She complained that I did not work fast enough. She followed me as I hauled it up the hill. When I got near the top I was tired and let the cart slip back while I caught my breath. A few lumps of manure rolled to the ground. She struck me on the back of my legs with the bamboo stake.

"Clumsy oaf! Miserable weakling! You pick up every speck of that compost!"

After making it clear that the horseshit mattered more to her than I did, she went back to the house. I worked dedicatedly, trying to rise in her estimation. When she drove off to meet Peter she did not even look my way.

It was just getting dark when she returned. She came to see how far I'd progressed. I had finished spreading the compost and was in the midst of turning the first of the other piles. My arms and legs ached. My back was breaking. I had accomplished a considerable amount but not as much as she expected.

"Not finished yet, you lazy thing?"

I swore I had not slacked off for a moment.

"You'll stay out here until you're finished. I don't care if it takes you all night."

I pleaded with her to allow me to continue tomorrow.

She gave a mocking laugh. "I don't know what's wrong with me. I must be going soft. All right. You can go to your room. I will see you at eight o'clock tomorrow morning. Bring me the Sunday paper along with my coffee."

I thanked her for her indulgence. I bathed and collapsed on my bed, too exhausted to write. I fell asleep in a blissful rapture, thinking of my beautiful and cruel Mistress.

Sunday was a brilliant, clear day.

"Will there be anything else, Madam?" I asked after I drew back her curtains to let the sunshine in. "Or shall I resume turning the compost?"

"Let that wait a bit," she yawned. "Today I want you to prepare a champagne brunch. Mrs Eblis, Mrs Harrod, Miss Thorndyke and her husband will be coming. Prepare extra food. As a diversion, Mrs Eblis and Mrs Harrod will be bringing their boys along."

I had not yet met Miss Thorndyke but I had heard about her. She was married to an investment banker named William Slate. The chairman of the boardroom was a wimp in the bedroom. Miss Thorndyke — she insisted on keeping her own name — had a reputation for being a severe disciplinarian, rougher on her husband than her friends were on their houseboys.

Mrs Eblis arrived first, shortly after eleven. She was with a muscular young man who wore a sleeveless shirt, shorts and a leather collar. Like my Mistress, Mrs Eblis was from the old school. She believed in depriving her servant of a name. *Boy* was identity enough for him. He stood behind her at attention. He seemed very anxious. Mrs Eblis complained to my Mistress that her boy had burned his hand while preparing her morning tea and shouted "Shit!". His filthy mouth greatly offended her and she wanted to teach him to mind his tongue in a way he would not forget. She asked if my Mistress could think of an appropriate punishment. My Mistress turned to me and told me to fetch a fresh bar of soap from her bath. When I brought the fine-milled, rose-scented French *savon*, she walked up to Mrs Eblis's boy and ordered him to open his mouth. When he did so reluctantly, she put the bar of soap squarely between his lips.

"Shit!" she shouted in his face.

She ordered him to stand behind his Mistress as she ate lunch. He had to be careful neither to salivate nor swallow.

Mrs Harrod appeared wearing a leopard-print sarong and a dozen silver bracelets on her right arm. She had two boys, a blond in chauffeur's livery and a black who wore tights that matched her sarong and had a gold ring in his nose. She called them by their pet names. The blond was Prince and the black Felix. On her cue, they sat obediently at her feet.

Miss Thorndyke and her husband arrived. She was a queen-sized woman, at least six feet tall and weighing close to two hundred pounds. She had a proud face and she carried herself beautifully. Her hair was long and flowing. Every element of her style was designed to make her seem even larger than she was. She wore dramatic makeup, chunky jewelry, a billowy blouse with a plunging neckline and tight stretch pants. William was thin, pale and rather short. He had a sunken chest, a turtle face and a sad, fragile look in his eyes. When his buxom wife raised a hand to smooth her hair, he flinched. I noticed he had bruises on his arms.

Miss Thorndyke did not introduce her husband to the other women. Thoroughly henpecked, William bowed and smiled timidly. He was allowed to sit at the table, but he kept his eyes down on his plate.

The women drank champagne. I brought out the food and, as always, kept the wine coming. Mrs Harrod asked me for an extra plate which she used to set a generous portion of bacon and eggs down for Felix. She took several bites from an apple and threw what was left on the ground for Prince. She had him on a diet, she explained.

My Mistress embarrassed me by complaining about what a slow gardener I was.

"Burke darling," said Mrs Harrod, "you can have Prince for the rest of the day to help your boy finish his chores.

And if your boy is slow, send him to me tomorrow. I'll get him up to speed."

While I opened the third bottle of champagne, Mrs Eblis turned to her boy. By now, with the soap in his mouth, his saliva was thoroughly sudsy and bubbling around his lips. She pinched his cheeks. He squirmed until he could take it no longer. The three women laughed as he spit out the soap and began to scrape his tongue with his fingernails trying to clear his mouth of the awful taste. William watched with an appalled look. He began to say something, but a sharp look from his wife was enough to make him remain silent.

The frivolity continued when Mrs Harrod commanded Felix to lie face up on the stone patio. She placed the sole of her sandal on his privates and commanded him to ejaculate. The women tittered and cheered as they watched Felix jerk in a spasm of ecstacy and spill his libidinous relish on the sole of his Mistress's shoe.

Mrs Harrod was not finished. She ordered Prince out of his uniform and to stand at ten paces. She removed the silver bracelets from her arms and passed them out, three to each woman. Prince put up a handsome erection, long and sleek. They used it as the peg for a game of ring toss.

As wild as my fantasies about sporting women, this demonstration of lewdness was more brazen than anything I had imagined. I felt terrified and excited about what they would do next.

"Boy!" my Mistress snapped her fingers at me.

I bowed to her.

"Yes, Madam."

"Undress!"

Unable to disobey, I took off my clothes. There was a chill in the September air. But I shivered more from embarrassment.

"What can you do to entertain us?" she asked.

"Let's see him dance!" Mrs Harrod demanded.

I hesitated.

"Now!" my Mistress shouted, clapping loudly in time.

I began to sway my hips. I was not very graceful. All the better for them. They laughed and applauded.

The fun ended abruptly when Mrs Thorndyke looked at her watch and announced that she was supposed to be at Myra Teufel's to see a horse she was thinking of buying. Mrs Eblis was quite tipsy. She had to lean on her boy as she walked to her car. Mrs Harrod took Felix to drive her and left Prince for my Mistress.

Before my Mistress retired to her room, she had Prince strip to his shorts and told him he was to help me with my chores. She ordered us not to speak to one another.

"You're on your honor as servants," she said. "And if one of you says a word to the other, don't think I won't know. You'll both wear clothespins on your tongues for a week."

In silence Prince and I went to the compost piles.

When we were away from the house, behind the hedge, Prince turned to me and said, "Do you feel your Mistress has a sixth sense, that she knows whether you've been bad or good."

"Yes, I do," I admitted. "She'll look at me and know if we spoke."

"And do you believe that there is honor in being a good servant?"

"I'm proud to be in my Mistress's service," I said. "Are you?"

Prince bobbed his head noncommittally. He said that seven years ago he was an aspiring actor working as a waiter in a New York City restaurant which Mrs Harrod frequented. He had an admitted weakness for older women and became smitten with her. She took a liking to him and engaged him to work for her.

"When I first came to Mrs Harrod's employ, honor still meant something to me," he said. "Hoping to please her, I did my best to obey her every wish, her every whim, but my best was never good enough. She reprimanded me continually. I tried to read her mind and think as I thought she wanted me to think. But with her unpredictable nature, this too was impossible. She would beat me for any slight infraction. As the years passed, I realized that my Mistress simply enjoyed inflicting pain, just as I enjoyed receiving it. It was in her nature to punish me, and it was in my nature to be punished. But when she punished me severely without cause, she felt guilty. She did not want me to be *too* good. In fact she wanted me to be bad sometimes so she could feel superior and justified in her disciplinary measures.

"A slave can only be acceptable if he is unacceptable: that's what I learned."

I worried about where I stood in my Mistress's estimation. If I did not make the grade, I felt I would shrivel and die. I wanted to perfect. But was perfection what she wanted?

Prince said that he no longer took himself seriously as an actor. His life was to serve Mrs Harrod. He said that he loved her very much and he felt that she loved him in return, although she had never said so or did anything to indicate this being the case.

Of course he was jealous of his Mistress's dalliances. "It took me time to learn to control my emotions," he went on. "Any display of rivalry only causes my Mistress to neglect me more. And she can be very heartless in that regard. On the other hand, she wants to know that separation from her is the unbearable punishment she intends it to be. I once flew into a jealous rage in which I turned over a table and broke three dishes. To punish me, she had me on my knees for an entire summer, working in the patio garden, a faceless, nameless serf, while she received male visitors. She bought Felix from Mrs Rosen. I was so desperate to stay in her good graces that I gladly took the punishment, looking forward to the day when she would deem my transgressions atoned for and take me back in her intimate service."

"And did she?"

"Eventually, but only after she had put me through a hell of jealousy and discomfort. Even now, Felix is her favorite. She treats me as if I am hardly worthwhile."

I confessed to him similar terror of what my Mistress might do.

"It's a hard life most of the time," he said, "and I've tried to quit. But my Mistress is inside me. She dominates my thoughts from within."

I knew what he meant. I enjoyed being in my Mistress's presence, however she treated me.

I also enjoyed working with Prince. I admired his strength and stamina. All he had to eat that day was an apple core, yet he shovelled and talked with the same effortless rhythm. His candor was contagious. I had so much to talk about. I told him I was with Lady Ketchener exactly a week and, new to the life, was surprised by the boldness of the ladies' diversions. I asked him if they often carried on as they did today.

"Too often," he replied.

Prince told me that it was customary and considered fair game for these women to poach one another's servants. Generally the poacher leaves her signature in some form on the boy's body. It was a goad to retaliation. Of course the servant who has allowed such a transgression on his Mistress's private property was severely punished by his Mistress.

I asked him if my Mistress had had him.

"Oh yes," he replied, "on several occasions. I caught hell from *my* Mistress for it."

"Will she have you today?" My jealousy made me choke on the question.

He told me that while a boy was "on loan", it was considered unsportswomanlike conduct to despoil him.

He told me to watch my step around Miss Thorndyke. She was the worst and most unfair. He said she had a taste for blood. He had heard through the grapevine that on one occasion she beat William so severely she put him in the hospital. "She regularly loses her temper and strikes out at her staff," Prince said. "I've heard that she has a private doctor to attend to the messes she makes when her temper flares and has spent a fortune in secret settlements, paying off her victims not to press charges.

"She sometimes puts her evil eye on me, and when she does I avoid her like the plague. So far I've stayed one step ahead of her."

It took us the remainder of the afternoon to turn the manure. We mixed in leaves, soil, grass clippings and kitchen waste. It was gratifying to see it done well.

Afterwards, we both reported to my Mistress. We had to wait until she finished bathing.

"Didn't I tell you two not to speak?"

We both nodded apologetically.

She pinned a note that said *Blabbermouth* on Prince's shirt and sent him home in the van to Mrs Harrod.

She turned to me. I tried to explain that I was only human and that Prince was good company. Conversation made the work go more smoothly.

"Quiet!" She cut me off, boxed my ears, put her hand in my mouth, and pinched my tongue with her thumbnail. "Don't you say another word! Isn't your Mistress enough *company* for you?"

She took me by the tongue, down the stairs, through the great room and into the kitchen. There was a room behind the pantry with a thick oak floor and a hatchdoor with a big brass bolt on it. I had investigated it a few days earlier. It was an old root cellar. She made me kneel down, slide back the bolt and open the door. When I did so, I felt the sole of her shoe on my back. With a push of her foot, she sent me flying forward into the blackness.

I fell several feet and landed uninjured on a dirt floor. She slammed the door on top of me and I heard her bolt it.

Stunned, I lay still. It took a few minutes for my eyes to adjust. Even so, my Mistress's oubliette was so dark I could barely see. The chamber had a low ceiling. I had to crawl on my hands and knees to explore. It was a rectangular space, about four feet by ten. In one corner I found a jug of water. A small sip told me it was potable. Near it, there was a plastic pail. I guessed it was for my eliminations.

I slept. I woke. There was no way to tell if it was night or day. No doubt Monday had come. I had been at Lavender Hill for a week. Every minute in the oubliette seemed like an hour. As I crawled restlessly with the centipedes, spiders and waterbugs, I did nothing but think of my Mistress, her soft, fragrant flesh and her luxurious bed. My longing was unbearable.

When she finally came to unbolt the dungeon door it was Tuesday morning. I squinted in the sunlight as I poked my head out of the darkness. She stood over me in her boots and riding pants. I was happier to see her than I was to see the sun, happier to breathe her perfume than to breathe fresh air. I praised her benevolence, told her how much I missed her and begged her pardon for talking to Prince.

"I realize it was wrong. It will never happen again. I promise."

"For your sake, it had better not. Now you smell foul. Clean up and get yourself something to eat. You have an hour. I'm lending you to Mrs Harrod as reimbursement for the loan of her boy. Prince needs help painting a fence."

I did as I was told and in an hour Prince came by in the Lavender Hill van. Mrs Harrod's response to our transgression was to have both his lips pierced and sealed by a small gold ring and a tiny padlock to which she kept the key. We drove to her estate in silence, our eyes on the road.

It was warm for a mid-September day. Mrs Harrod was sunning herself on the pool deck, chatting on the telephone. Felix was lying naked on a towel next to her. He was erect. She was idly touching him, teasing him. Prince and I painted the picket fence around the flower garden. After a while Mrs Harrod took Felix inside.

When Prince and I finished, it was nearly dark. I drove home in the van. We had spent the day together and neither of us had said a word to the other.

I woke early in the morning and recorded my latest experiences. When I brought my Mistress her coffee, she ordered me into bed with her. She had me feel her. Her nipples were firm. Her puss was wet. She pushed me down to smell her candy musk. I became feverish with desire. She reminded me that she owned me and handled me in a very imposing way. She tied the silk belt from her robe around my scrotum and amused herself by pulling me this way and that. I had to be very fast in order to avoid being hurt.

She pushed me on my back, put the belt around my neck and twisted it to deny me air. She lay on me and took me inside her. I looked at her face. In the full flush of pleasure, she became divinely beautiful. Totally at her mercy, I jerked in spasms of pleasure even as I gasped for breath.

Looking at her, feeling her on me, engulfed in her scent, I would have been content to die then and there.

Abruptly, she released the belt and looked at her appointment book.

"Call the salon and confirm my appointment at ten," she said coldly. Her enjoyment was not complete until she made me feel how little I mattered to her. "That will be all."

My Mistress bathed, dressed and went out. She was not gone ten minutes when Mrs Eblis made an unexpected call. She was dressed in gold chains, a short black silk shirt-dress and alligator shoes. I told her that my Mistress had gone to the salon. I expected she would return in an hour. I asked Mrs Eblis if she would like to wait. She said she would and ordered me to bring a pot of coffee to the parlor.

I served the coffee and asked if there was anything else she needed. She directed me to bring her a pitcher of water. When I returned, she was standing, looking out the window, pouring herself a second cup of coffee. I set the water down on the table and turned to leave. Mrs Eblis moved between me and the door, blocking my exit.

"Will there be anything else, Ma'am?"

"No, I have everything I want."

She took a step closer to me. It was not clear what she intended.

"Will you be kind enough to excuse me, Ma'am? I have my Mistress's bed to make and her room to tidy."

"You are a good boy, aren't you?"

"I try to be, Ma'am. If my Mistress comes home and sees a mess, it'll put her in a bad mood."

"Oh, will it? And if you were rude to her guest?"

"My Mistress would not like that either."

She put down her cup.

"Pour me some water and bring it here." She sat on the love seat.

I did as I was told.

"And what if I told your Mistress you tried to get fresh with me? What would she do with you then?"

"I'm sure she'd be very angry."

"She'd cut your balls off."

I had to wince.

"Now take off your clothes and be quick about it. If you don't do as I say, I'll tell your Mistress a tale that will be the end of you."

I was worried about what my Mistress would do if she found out about this. The thought of being unloyal to my Mistress made me feel despicable and dirty inside. But I was frightened of Mrs Eblis. I didn't doubt she would make good on her threat. And, like my Mistress, she was used to having what she wanted, and without delay. I felt helpless, powerless to resist.

As I removed my shirt, pants, shoes and shorts, Mrs Eblis drank two more glasses of water.

When I was naked, she ordered me to lie face up on the piano bench. She poured herself yet another cup of coffee.

While she sipped it, she lifted her leg over the bench and stood over me with her knees apart. I could see all the way up her smooth tan legs. She was not wearing panties. The lips of her vagina, like petals of a pink rose, were moist and slightly open. She was a natural blond.

I felt ashamed. I turned my head.

"You *are* a good boy, aren't you?" she said.

Mrs Eblis sat on me. I felt her lower lips tickling the mouse I had promised belonged only to my Mistress. My heart wanted to be true to my Mistress, but the mouse was ruled by the heat of the moment. Born prey, it poked up its head and Mrs Eblis swallowed it in her nether mouth.

I did not put up a struggle, nor did I pitch in wildly. Mrs Eblis grew irritated by my reserve. "I know you love it, boy," she said. "Let me see you show it! Move!"

To prod me she began to scratch my chest and shoulders with her sharp fingernails. She growled and spit like a wild cat when she approached her climax. I could not control myself. I shook and twitched as I came inside her.

I closed my eyes. I didn't want to look at my assailant. I wanted to forget what had just happened. She reached for the glass and took a long drink of water. I hoped she had gotten what she wanted and would go. But she was not through with me. She moved up on the bench and soaked my face in my own semen and her puss's juices. She had me lick her ass.

"Now fuck me, again, you little cock." She wiggled my limp member. When it did not immediately stiffen, she began to knead my plums and squeeze them impatiently.

She hurt me and made me afraid. Tears came to my eyes.

"Does your Mistress put up with such slacking off?" she demanded. She slapped me twice, palm and backhand, across the face. I tried to move but she grabbed my hair and held my head under her. Suddenly I felt a warm torrent in my mouth, nose, eyes and ears. It soaked my hair and ran down my chest. She laughed wildly and shrieked with pleasure as she pissed every drop of the pot of coffee and the pitcher of water on me. When she was finished, she took an atomizer of perfume from her purse and sprayed me both in the face and in the crotch. The fragrance stung my eyes and the tip of my penis. I fell to the floor and cried loudly.

"On second thought," she said with a bored yawn, "I don't think I'll wait for your Mistress." She threw her scarf down. "Give her my regards. No need to show me out."

After she departed, I tried to get up but the attack left me stunned. An hour passed. I don't know where it went. I did not hear my Mistress enter. Suddenly she was standing over me, perfectly coiffed.

"What happened here?" She sniffed. "I know that perfume. What's this scarf doing here? Rene! And what is this wet spot? Why, you little slut! I can't leave you alone for a minute."

I begged her not to send me away.

"Bad boy!" My Mistress kicked me, grabbed me by the hair, and pushed me face-down in Mrs Eblis's pee. She was wearing new boots with sharp heels and pointed toes. She put her toe between my buttocks and dug her heel into the backs of my thighs.

"What kind of servant will you make if I can't leave you alone in the house?"

Before she left for lunch, she threw me into the oubliette.

Several days later, Miss Thorndyke and Mrs Harrod joined my Mistress for breakfast on the patio. When they were finished eating, Mrs Harrod asked my Mistress if she might have a tour of the gardens. The roses had come into their September bloom. My Mistress asked Miss Thorndyke if she would like to join them, but Miss Thorndyke looked at her watch.

"I'll take the tour another time, darling. William's in Los Angeles this week. It's eight o'clock there, the perfect time to check up on him. May I use your phone?"

"Of course, darling. You'll have privacy in the library. Boy, show Miss Thorndyke to the telephone."

I escorted Miss Thorndyke through the house to the study. Instead of picking up the telephone, Mrs Thorndyke turned to me and, without warning, took me in her arms and kissed me. "Let's see how quickly you can do it, boy!" she said as her big hands brazenly tugged at my zipper.

I was still bruised from the punishment I received for allowing Mrs Eblis's poaching. I pulled away.

"Please, Ma'am, I beg you," I said, "I belong to my Mistress. She takes very unkindly to my being used by other women. I hope you will respect her wishes. I feel I must."

Miss Thorndyke was my height and had a weight advantage on me. She pulled me close and kissed me again. When I did not respond but went limp in her arms, she became furious.

"How dare you refuse me! You little slave-prick, I'll have your ass for this!" She punched me in the stomach and knocked the wind out of me. She ran to the window and shouted, "Burke, Lilith, darlings, help. Hurry!"

My Mistress and Mrs Harrod quickly returned to see what the matter was.

"What have you been teaching your boy, darling?" Miss Thorndyke said. "He tried to get fresh."

Of course my Mistress must have known that Miss Thorndyke was lying, but she chose not to offend her friend by questioning the allegation. The poaching game went on. My Mistress had been had. She was a sore loser, but she would not show it. She glowered at me. My stomach clenched and my jaw stiffened. I broke out in a cold sweat, fearful of what would happen next.

"I want to see this boy punished," said Miss Thorndyke.

"Boy, get me my crop," my Mistress said.

"No, darling," said Miss Thorndyke, "you're too easy on him.

Let me handle him. I guarantee he won't be doing this again."

Remembering what Prince told me about Miss Thorndyke's brutality, I fell to my knees in front of my Mistress and begged that she punish me herself.

"So you admit it, boy?" said my Mistress. "Why must you be such a slut? Yes, Thalia darling, do what you like with him. Kill him, for all I care! Come, darling," she said, turning to Mrs Harrod. "You wanted to see the roses?"

I was terrified being left alone with Miss Thorndyke. She looked down, her eyes expressionless, her mouth set in a hard smile. I cowered at her feet. The big woman seemed to get bigger. She grabbed me by my hair and led me out.

Her car was a sporty two-seater. She pushed me into the passenger side and she got behind the wheel.

She drove very fast and handled the car recklessly, taking the curves on Swamp Road without braking or even down-shifting. I felt at any moment the car might go out of control. She had only one hand on the wheel. When her right hand was not on the stick, it was on me, squeezing me with her fleshy, large palm and scratching me with her sharp nails. I could feel that she had plenty of experience and knew just where to touch for pleasure as well as for pain. She did not say a word to me and I sat terrified, trying without success to maintain silence. My voice shifted between sighs of pleasure when she stroked me, cries of pain when she pinched me, and nervous whimpers about her driving.

Miss Thorndyke lived in Waldgrave. Under normal circumstances it was a fifteen minute drive west of Norbury. Miss Thorndyke made it in ten. Her house was large, built in the eighteen-nineties by a lumber baron. She pulled up to the garage and ordered me out.

My heart was skipping beats as she took me to a sunny spot in the garden where there was a pergola. The sets of parallel, upright wooden posts were connected by cross beams and covered with climbing roses. A tall, well-built woman, wearing work boots and overalls with nothing under them, was at work, clipping the roses. She had short dark curly hair and a delicate face. Her breasts were large and firm. They bulged over the denim. Her underarms were unshaved.

She greeted Miss Thorndyke with a kiss. Miss Thorndyke stroked her breasts.

"Nina, this is Burke Ketchener's boy," said Miss Thorndyke. "He had the nerve to get fresh with me. Burke has given him to me to set straight."

Nina smiled contemptuously at me. "Poor bitch," she barked. "You've messed with the wrong women."

Miss Thorndyke motioned with her head. At the top of the pergola, between two of the uprights, attached to a beam, was a thick brass chain, outfitted with adjustable leather straps and padlocks. Seeing the whipping post made my blood run cold. I tried to run but Nina grabbed me. With Miss Thorndyke's help, she dragged me by my arms and used the chain to secure my hands over my head with my back to the sun.

I dangled helplessly as Nina ripped off my shirt and Miss Thorndyke pulled my pants down to my ankles. She borrowed Nina's hand clipper and pressed the sharp, cold steel blade to my privates. She meant to scare me and succeeded. I started to plead again, as if for my life.

Miss Thorndyke looked at me with disdain. "Shush!" she hissed. She removed the silk handkerchief from the breast pocket of her blazer and pushed it in my mouth to gag me. It tasted of her perfume.

"We'll attend to him later," said Miss Thorndyke. "Come now, Nina, let me fix you some lunch."

The two women went off. I was left in the sun. The rose bushes grew close on either side. If I shifted my position even an inch the nasty branches pricked and scratched my skin. The wind picked up. A heavy, thorny cane broke loose from its tie on the cross-beam and fell directly on my head. Every gust brushed it across my scalp. By late afternoon, my backside, unused to being exposed to the heat of day, felt as if it were on fire. The bruise my Mistress made on my shoulder still had not healed. It began to throb.

My physical discomfort was nothing compared to what I was going through inside. My thoughts were like tenterhooks. I was unnerved by what Miss Thorndyke planned to do. But I was more tormented by the realization that in all likelihood I had failed my trial with my Mistress.

Toward the end of the day, two women in black and white serving uniforms came out. One told the other what I was accused of. The second gasped with disapproval.

"Don't worry," said the first, "the animal's going to get what he deserves."

The two women then began bustling about the lawn, setting up a bar and bringing out a spread of hors d'oeuvres. There was going to be a party.

Mrs Eblis arrived first with Prince and Felix. Then Mrs Rosen came with her boyfriend. Finally Madame Bayard and Mrs Oistereich, the two old witches, arrived. Each had a young man, following her. I was to be an example of what happens to boys who forget their place and try to force themselves on a woman. One by one the women came up behind me, pinched my raw buttocks and told me how despicable I was. The humiliation was crushing. My Mistress arrived last with a young man. She introduced him as Phillipe and said he was on trial as her new boy. My sense of loss was so devastating I hoped Miss Thorndyke would kill me.

All the women had a couple of drinks. They were in a good mood and eager for the entertainment to start. Finally Miss Thorndyke appeared. I caught a glimpse of her over my shoulder. Larger than life, she was dressed in a soft silk suit and heels. There seemed nothing menacing about her. She greeted everyone with a kiss and a "Hello, darling".

Then Nina came out of the house, dressed in a hooded cape, black tights and black velvet boots. She wore a grotesque, theatrical mask and was holding a whip that consisted of three leather strips attached to a wooden handle. Each lash had a piece of bone tied to the end. My blood froze as she stepped up to me. A hush fell on the gathering.

She hit me lightly. She merely flicked her wrist but I could feel the pieces of bone. They stung and caused me to jump. The roses pricked me in a dozen places.

"Boy," she growled, "If you're honest, I'll go easy on you. I want you to tell everyone exactly why you're here."

I was there because I refused Miss Thorndyke's advance. But I couldn't say that.

Nina hit me again. This time a little harder. I started to cry.

"Admit your crime," she said. "Clear your conscience. You'll feel better. And I will go easier on you."

Even though I was innocent, I confessed to making a pass at Miss Thorndyke. I promised her I had learned my lesson. So earnest were my apologies, even I forgot that I did not do what I was accused of.

My admission seemed to incense rather than assuage Miss Thorndyke. She took the whip from Nina and struck me across my buttocks with the full force of her big arms. The blow was so painful I saw stars. I jerked and scratched my forehead on the branches. Blood ran down my brow. The men sighed and the women laughed.

She turned the lashing back to Nina, who laid into me with a fury, striking me repeatedly without mercy. Every blow burned more than the one before. I passed beyond pain to a mild state of shock. As if in a dream, I heard Mrs Rosen and Mrs Harrod, no doubt frightened about being accomplices to such an assault, come forward and plead with Miss Thorndyke to stop it.

Miss Thorndyke called for a vodka-tonic with a twist. She spent a few moments adding agony to the injuries Nina had caused me by rubbing the slice of lemon into my wounds.

I remained in this position for another hour, often crying in pain and from the disgrace. At seven-thirty guests began leaving. Every woman came up behind me and added her chastisement. They called me a jelly fish, a pig, a snake in the grass and dumb prick.

My Mistress tweaked the bruise on my shoulder and opened up the scab. "You've only gotten half of what you deserve," she hissed. "When I get you home, I'm going to give you the rest."

I had assumed she would not want me back. I thanked her for giving me a another chance to prove myself. I promised she would not regret it.

"We'll see if you can be motivated by a little competition to serve me," she said. She ordered Phillipe to bring the car around.

Nina had the two uniformed women take me down. and drive me back to Lavender Hill. Unable to sit on my swollen behind, I lay on my stomach across the back seat. The thought that I was going back to Lavender Hill, even if it was just so my Mistress could punish me, even if I had to share her with Phillipe, was an overwhelming joy.

My joy was short-lived. She sent me to my room, but saw to it that the doors between us were opened. I had to endure her laughing and groaning with pleasure and Phillipe's voice, raised with excitement, as she played with him. The sounds hurt more than the punishment inflicted by the savage Miss Thorndyke.

The next day there was a slight chill in the air and the maples were in their first faint blush of autumn.

When I ventured to bring my Mistress her coffee, I was relieved to see no sign of Phillipe. She had sent him off to sleep in the guest house. Whenever she had a man in her bed, she always had me change the sheets. I asked her if she wished me to do so this morning.

She was short with me. "When I want something done, I will tell you. Go sweep the tennis court."

There was a tennis court on my Mistress's property but I had never seen her use it. This morning she summoned Phillipe and challenged him to a match. I had never seen her play, but I had the idea from various conversations that she was rather good. Indeed, she was a fierce competitor. However, it so happened that Phillipe, who worked as a lowly ballboy at the Arcadian Club, was better. He did not have the sense to throw the match.

She could not abide the idea that a plaything of hers could beat her. I'm sure that in front of everyone at the club she appeared the best of sports, but she was, in fact, infuriated by defeat. When Phillipe went to shake her hand after his last point, she called him a cheat and ordered him to leave. I was glad to see him go. She would take her aggravation out on me.

She reprimanded me for not sweeping the court carefully enough.

"I lost the match because of bad hops," she said. "And why were you standing there gawking instead of putting fresh linens on my bed?"

I had a kneejerk reaction to defend myself. I pointed out that she specifically told me not to do so.

"Liar!" She stamped her foot. "Disrespectful whelp! What's becoming of you? You take liberties with my friends and now you talk back to me."

Even though I knew I had done no such thing, I begged her forgiveness. She accused me of patronizing her. She was most beautiful when she was angry. When I assured her I idolized her, she struck me across the face with the back of her hand.

I felt ashamed, small, unmanned. Yet my renegade flesh made a spectacle of itself.

She sat in the chaise and asked me to bring her a towel. The day was warm and she was perspiring freely. While she dried her face she asked me to take off her tennis shoes. I fell to my knees and did so without delay.

At her feet I felt the highest bliss.

Without looking at me, she put her big toe to my lips and thrust it in.

"Suck, boy!" she commanded.

She took plain enjoyment in my slavering devotion and her own elevated position. She put her hand into her tennis dress and played with her puss. She did not take long to reach climax. She dozed for a few moments with a contented smile. But the effect of sexual satisfaction was brief. She awoke in a mood more foul than before.

"Why are you sitting there, Mouse? Didn't I order you to remake my bed?"

I scrambled upstairs and did her bidding. When I came back down, she was still sitting on the patio with an angry expression.

She pointed out tiny weeds growing between the bricks and ordered me to pull them out. She would not let me wear knee pads or gloves. She paced around me, smoking cigarettes, making threats. Then she went into the house. After an hour, my knees were breaking and my knuckles and fingertips were bloody and sore. She came out with a metal canister. She shook it in front of my face. Something rattled inside.

"Follow me, boy."

She took me to part of the garden where ivy and low evergreen shrubs were growing. She removed the lid from the tin and showed me what was making the clatter: marbles.

"There are three hundred here," she said, "and there better be three hundred here at the end of the day." And with that she took the marbles by the handful and cast them into the dense ground cover.

My punishment, an impossible and senseless task, was to collect every marble and put it back in the canister.

I worked until late in the afternoon but I only collected two hundred and thirty-five. It was getting dark, hard to see. Late summer, the air became cool. A light rain began to fall. I came into the house. She was sitting by the fire, reading. I begged her to allow me to resume my search in the morning. But she told me I was to continue. I would find some rain gear and a flashlight in the mudroom.

The drizzle turned to a steady rain. The wind picked up. In the dark, I searched under every branch and leaf and felt every inch of muddy earth. At eleven o'clock, I had only come up with two hundred and eighty-seven, although I covered the whole area several times. The lights went off in the parlor. A few moments later they went on in her bedroom. I saw her undressing in the window.

She turned off her lights shortly after midnight. I finally stopped looking. There were no more, I decided. I suspected she knew. I went up to my quarters by the back stairs, stripped off my wet clothes, and crawled under the covers, shivering, hating her and loving her.

The rain continued the next morning. When I brought her coffee, she took me into her bed and played with me. She let me come inside her. I expected her to dismiss me as she always did after I had served my purpose, but today she held me in her embrace, put her soft lips to my ear and whispered, "I love you."

The words made me ecstatic. They prompted an imme-diate physical reaction and she took me in her again. For the remainder of the morning, she held me in her bed. She told me she loved me again and again, and each time I heard those words I went into her with more ardor than I ever dreamed possible. By noon I had risen to the peak of love eight times. Before lunch she began another round of sweet talk and fondling. She wanted me again.

Although my spirit was willing, my flesh was weak. When she could not instantly get another rise out of me, she pressed her knee into my groin and reprimanded me for not loving her enough. She reminded me that I was lucky to be hers, that there were dozens of other boys eager to take my place.

"You must try harder, or, as much as I love you, I'll have to let you go."

The admonishment was enough to stiffen me. She took me for the ninth time.

The following day she went shopping and then to lunch. She came home late in the afternoon. I was placing fresh flowers in her room. She snatched me by my hair, pushed me down, pulled up her skirt and had me sniff her. She had not bathed since the evening before. Her mouse trap smelled like the tiger cage at the zoo. The full-bodied animal scent affected my brain. I became a quivering mass of jelly at her feet. I craved release but she would not allow it.

She dismissed me with the strict order not to ejaculate. She threatened to terminate my employment if I spilled even a drop. The Goddess knew my every thought and action. I dared not displease her. I spent the night tossing and turning, but keeping my continence.

I rose early, wrote, bathed and groomed myself. I went to bring my Mistress her coffee. She inspected me carefully by palming my plums, soft and overripe. She raised her hand up and down as if to judge their weight. Satisfied that I was heavier than yesterday, she toyed with me further until she had roused even greater proof of my feelings. Then she had me stand and watch as she came by her own hand.

"Dismissed!" she said, waving me away after she had finished. "And don't you dare even think about touching yourself. The load you're carrying is for me."

She went to lunch with Mrs Eblis. She had dinner plans with Peter, but shortly before she was to go out, I heard her shouting on the telephone. She was fighting with Peter. She cancelled her plans. I was happy to hear it. I served her a light supper and cleaned the kitchen.

Before she went to bed, she summoned me to her lair and had me kneel by her bedpost while she undressed. I humbly offered to help her off with her shoes and stockings if she would be so kind as to stretch out her feet to me. She mocked me even as she allowed me the privilege. She stood back and tossed her panties my way. I fell on them for a whiff of her. The luscious, musty, meaty essence that collected in those delicate folds of silk and lace weakened me.

She gave me a wicked smile and picked up the telephone.

"Peter? I'm sorry. I was out sorts. It's this damn houseboy. I don't think he's working out. Can I invite you for a nightcap? Say, in an hour?"

Again she dismissed me with the injunction that I was not to release my love. I begged her to have mercy. "You're torturing me," I cried.

She took me by my hair, led me to my room and locked me in. I lay in bed, tormented by jealousy, wrestling with temptation. The prolonged excitement gave me a lasting erection. Hoping to be master of myself and acceptable to my Mistress, I repeated my prayer to the Muse. Eventually I drifted into dreams of disappointment and frustration.

In the morning I was still highly on edge. My manfruit's condition had grown even more touch and go. But, having not succumbed to temptation, I felt the Goddess was with me. I sat at my desk and what was damned up in one place flowed in another. I added juicy details to my true confession of being a love slave.

The torment lasted for six days. On the seventh day, the first of autumn, when I brought my Mistress her coffee, she grabbed my hand and drew me to her under the covers.

I lay still, silent as a mouse, while she played with herself. Need had made my senses keen. I was enthralled by her warmth, the heavy scent of her body and the motion she made with her hips. Then she took me on top of her and pulled me inside her. She looked up at me. Her eyes sparkled. She said she loved me. I wanted to die in her arms. This was heaven. It was what I lived for.

She held me tight, reached down behind my back and between my legs and gave my swag a light slap. "Now!" she growled, beginning to shake. "Give me all you have!"

She arched her back, stiffened and trembled under me as if an electric shock passed through her body. My passion, so hard and long after a week of frustration, stormed. I was tossed on tempest waves of pleasure.

Afterwards, my heart leaped out to her. I felt we had shared a magic moment. Floating on a cloud of joy, I tried to kiss her, but she turned her head. She pushed me away.

"Dismissed!"

It was not easy pleasing a woman who was most pleased when she was displeased.

For days she ignored me completely. She was always on the run. She wanted to avoid examining her life and suffering because of her own shortcomings. I held her above all law and principles. She used my great sympathy for her to magically transfer to me the pain she wished to leave behind. As hard as it was to bear my Mistress's nasty moods, no pain was worse than being ignored. But because she had the power to give my life meaning or take it away, the more she neglected me, the more my affection for her rose.

I felt I was dying without her love. I prayed the urge would come over her and she would use me as her pleasure tool. When no such invitation came, I took austere pleasure submitting my will to hers. I practiced patience. I accepted my Mistress as she was, adorable yet heartless. I could not feel my innate inferiority without simultaneously feeling her tremendous, mysterious power.

Whenever I went to make up her room, I found she had gone through her wardrobe like a whirlwind, trying on dozens things and throwing them here and there. It took me hours to put all the clothing back from where it came. What could be more enchanting than picking up after my carefree love? The work, rather than distract me, kept her on my mind every moment.

I embraced my own function as an insignificant diversion. Who was *I* to demand *her* time or attention? However, my compliant devotion only seemed to increase the distance she put between us. Several more days passed. She came and went without even looking at me. One evening after she dashed off to dinner, I found her panties on her bedroom floor. I picked them up. They were warm and stained with fresh moisture.

I remembered what Prince told me: the basis of the dominant's pleasure is the worthlessness of the submissive. By being enduring and steady, displaying the patience of a saint, wasn't I challenging my Mistress to rethink her low estimation of me? I saw Prince's point. She wanted to know I was weak, that separation from her was the unbearable punishment she intended it to be.

When she returned, I could not control myself. I went into her room uninvited, holding the lacy treasure. She was sitting in bed, reading Guermantes. I fell to my knees before her, put the pants to my face and let my lower nature run its course unchecked.

She called me an insolent brat. She reached over and slapped me for my boldness. I felt alive again. She threatened to terminate me if I did not satisfy her immediately. But I needed no intimidation. A new, stiffer passion arose before the old wilted.

From then on, I decided to take her orders with a grain of salt. I understood too much obedience was a fault. When she was bad she was very bad. She wanted me to be just as bad once in a while, so she could feel superior.

My Mistress informed me that her Aunt Emma and her Uncle Max Peck were coming the following day and would be staying with her through the week. She told me that after I had done the errands, seen to it that the beds were made with fresh linens and the house was clean and well-stocked with food, I was to take the van, go to my room in the boarding house and stay there until she called me.

The worst punishment she could inflict was to banish me from her presence entirely. I begged her to put me in her oubliette where I at least would be comforted to know she was walking overhead.

"Obey me! Do not question!"

I felt angry as I drove off. I was tempted to take the car, go to the interstate and drive, but I would not get very far on the small allowance she had given me for food. Nor did I want to leave my Mistress. I was incapable of disobedience. I went back to my room at Mrs Gooden's as I had been instructed.

While the sun went down, I lay on the bed sulking. My Mistress's cruelty only made me want her more. I ejaculated into an old cotton bath robe. Physically and emotionally exhausted, I slept and did not wake until the next morning.

Although still pensive and sick at heart, I felt physically refreshed and mentally energetic. I unpacked my notebook and went to work adding details to my love-slave journal. While being in the presence of my Mistress always got me worked up, writing about her soothed me. The day seemed to pass in a few hours. One day I hoped to be taken seriously as a writer. And one day I hoped that my Mistress, seeing the love I had for her and the ardent way I admired her, would return my feelings as one human being to another.

At night I watched television and ate cheddar cheese, crackers and apples I bought at Emerson's. I imagined my Mistress enjoying the warmth of her blood relations. I felt desperately alone. Public Television, in the midst of a fund-raising drive, was showing a lecture by a self-help guru. He was warning the audience not to give away their power. "As you think, so you are," he repeated again and again as he invited the audience to take stock of their lives.

It was October 1. I had been in my Mistress's service for a month. Looking back, I suppose I should have been appalled by the way I let myself be treated, but then I felt the fever pitch of emotion she evoked. It was a thrill that gave my life meaning. Perhaps I was not in the best of mental health, but neither was I afraid to discover the full extent of my passion.

I passed the week in an exalted sorrow. On Sunday morning I decided to make a small departure from my tedious routine by treating myself to breakfast at The Round Table, a restaurant on Main Street in Norbury. I took a booth by the window. While I ate my eggs, I watched the congregation exit Sunday Service at Saint Andrew's Episcopal across the street. Among the flinty Protestants I saw a plain young woman dressed in a conservative suit and unflattering brown loafers. She was walking with an older couple. I could see a family resemblance. All three faces were set in puritanical, God-fearing expressions. As they neared the curb, I got a better look at the young woman. My heart stopped. Was it? Yes. On second inspection, I recognized her too well. I looked at the plates of the car she was unlocking: LHF 1. There was no mistake. This was my Mistress with her aunt and uncle.

She was perfect in the part of the severe Yankee Lady. This new conservative persona made the whole of who she was more exotic, more compelling to me. My heart broke as she drove off. I prayed she would call me back to Lavender Hill soon.

My prayers were answered at nine o'clock that night. Mrs Gooden said I had a call.

"Witch sounds drunk as a skunk," she commented.

"Auntie Emma and Uncle Max have gone," my Mistress said, slurring her words. "Thank goodness!"

On the way back to Lavender Hill my expectations rose. I felt rapture at the thought of being reunited with her. When I saw her, the signs of love were obvious to read in my face and below. But she seemed distraught. She was holding a glass of Scotch. She gulped it and snarled furiously at me, "You're a little whore! I'm not sure I want you anymore. I'm a respectable woman. You cheapen me."

"Please —"

"Shush! I said I'm not sure! Go back to the boarding house and wait while I decide."

"But —"

"An acceptable slave does not question!" she said sharply.

I felt crushed. I went back to the boarding house, lay on the bed and cried. After a while I began to see that maybe my Mistress was right. Maybe she was indeed respectable and I was the whore, the parasite. I felt fortunate I had this good woman willing to train me and beat the devil out of me, if necessary.

The following day, as penance, I devoted myself entirely to my true confession of love for my Mistress. I wrote numerous pages describing the experience of being with her. Late in the afternoon, as I was reviewing what I had written, making corrections, she called me. Again, she sounded as if she was under the influence.

"Having my Aunt and Uncle around may have put me out of sorts," she explained. She stopped short of apologizing. "Come home, boy! I can't wait to see you."

I showered, shaved and returned to Lavender Hill as fast as the speed limit would allow. I arrived just after sunset. There were no lights on. It seemed as if there was nobody home.

I entered the house. "Madam!" I called but received no answer. I went from room to room. Even before I saw her, I smelled her. She was sitting in the study by the fire, dressed in a silk robe and velvet slippers. There was a bottle on the table beside her. I flung myself at her feet and told her how much I missed her and what a privilege it was to serve her. I tried to kiss the hem of her robe. My grovelling provoked her contempt. She gave me a sudden poke in the mouth with her velvet toe.

I grunted in pain.

"Oops!" she said with mock sympathy. "Did I hurt you?"

"No, Madam."

She laughed coldly and told me I was a sorry excuse for a human being.

I did not argue.

"What have you been doing all week?" she asked.

"I've been writing," I answered timidly.

"Let me see." She put the lamp on. "Bring me your briefcase."

I got it from the hall where I had left it. I handed it to her. She opened it. On top were the pages I had written earlier that day.

"What's this?" she asked, glancing over the first paragraph. "Is this about me?"

When I began to reply, she stamped her foot. "Be quiet!" she snapped. "Sit!" She pointed to the floor beside where she sat.

I sat back on my haunches, hands in my lap, eyes on the floor. She lay back in her chair and began to read. Out of the corner of my eye, I saw her smile. Then she stroked her breasts. She seemed pleased. When she got to the page on which I described not recognizing her as she came out of Saint Andrew's, her expression changed to a stern frown. She made a fist and crumpled the manuscript.

"How dare you write about me!" she snarled. "How dare you pretend to know anything about me! I will never be as *you* expect me to be."

I told her I quite understood. I apologized.

"I was planning to have you help me with my social notes," she said, "but after reading this, I've changed my mind."

Disheartened, I reached for the ball of paper. "If it displeases you so, Madam, I will throw it into the fire."

She held it from me. "No," she said, "I want to keep it to remind me what an impudent little pup you are." She looked away from me. "Now go to your room. I'm still deciding whether to keep you or not."

I felt the excoriating pain of rejection. My heart broke. My blood boiled over with excitement. I begged her to allow me to ejaculate on the floor in front of her as a token of my great feeling for her. "At least, let me divert you for a moment. What harm will it cause *you*?"

"No! I find you oppressive."

"Please, Madam! Must you rob me of every shred of self-respect and have me beg like this."

She smiled mischievously. "Maybe I do deserve a little indulgence. Come here, *Mouse!*" she roared. "Let your Mistress feel how frightened of her you are!"

She took me in hand and laughed loudly as I quivered in holy dread, awed by her immense power.

The Columbus Day weekend was the busiest tourist time of the year around Norbury. The leaves on the beeches and sugar maples were red and gold. The antique dealers had their fall clearance sales. It was also the final three days of my six-week trial.

I was raking leaves in the twilight Friday evening when she left for dinner. She stopped her car, rolled down the window and said, "Now there's a good boy, using every moment of daylight to make yourself useful! Sometimes you surprise me, Mouse. And sometimes you can be so disappointing. I can't decide whether to keep you or not." She drove off.

I prayed to the Goddess that I was good enough to become a permanent part of Lady Ketchener's household. If she told me to go it would be like a death sentence.

My Mistress continued her overindulgence. On Saturday she started drinking at lunch. By evening she was a holy terror, unpredictable, restless, reckless and belligerent. Everything was my fault.

"Have you forgotten?" She pulled my hair and tossed my head from side to side. "I like to see you well-groomed. When are you going to learn how to look like a proper servant?"

The reason I existed was to please my Mistress, but often it was hard to know her wishes. "By 'well-groomed' do you mean you want me to keep my hair short?"

"I mean what I said, you sniveling worm," she slapped me. "It's up to you to read my mind. Do you understand?"

I nodded. "Yes, Madam. I think so."

"I don't think you do, stupid boy. When you are with me you must not think. I am your mind. I think for you. This is the hardest thing for you to learn."

She cancelled her dinner plans, poured herself a tall Scotch, grabbed me by the hair, and led me to her bedroom. I felt an elated terror, as if I had been sentenced to heaven and hell at the same time.

"On the bed, boy."

I lay naked on my back. She climbed on top of me and pinched my nipple until I cried in pain. When I tried to protect myself, she pinned my arms over my head. Of course, she was not strong enough to hold me, but I did not dare struggle. She had a large barrette in her hair. She removed it and showed me the interlocking rows of sharp plastic teeth that snapped closed on a tight spring.

"This would really hurt if I put it on your nipple . . ."

She gave me a gentle nip and I squirmed uncomfortably. "Please, Madam."

" . . .or on your plums!"

When I felt the clip at my stone fruit, I moaned an earnest plea.

I was relieved when she put it back in her hair and pinched my nipple again with her thumb. Glad for the lesser torture, I accepted the pain impassively.

"Over!" She snapped her fingers.

I rolled over on my stomach.

She lay belly down on my back and pressed her bush between my buttocks. Top dog to underdog, she whispered in my ear.

"You're a mutt! A bitch! Say it!"

"I'm a mutt, a bitch."

It thrilled her to hear me say it. She held me tight, sighed with excitement and commenced the stiff twitch that marked her orgasm.

I always felt the greatest honor to be near her while she trembled in ecstacy. Her transport gave me more pleasure than my own.

Sexual release did little to smooth her edginess, however. She ordered me to get a cigarette for her from the other room. I would have been happy to oblige, but she was still lying on top of me. I dared not buck her off. I waited. She started rubbing herself against me again. The alcohol caused her to forget her request. Once more her excitement escalated. Her second orgasm seemed to rock her more than the first. I felt my backside soaked with her sweat and her sweet and sour relish. Again, although I did not ejaculate, I experienced an overflow of love which left me feeling warm and happy, both weak and powerful at the same time.

Her pleasure subsided as quickly as it intensified. A moment after, she was already dissatisfied, looking for the next thrill.

"Where's the cigarette I asked for, you disobedient bitch." She slapped my head and rolled off my back. "Go fetch for your Mistress!"

I came back with the cigarette and lit it for her. She motioned me to sit at the foot of the bed.

"You don't think that your Mistress would actually hurt you, do you?" She inhaled and blew smoke in my face.

I did, but I dared not say so. I shrugged.

She glowered at me. "Obviously you do. Stupid bitch!" She picked up her Scotch and said, "This is poison."

She took a large swallow and began to cough.

"Water!" she demanded.

I quickly ran into her bath and returned with a glass of water.

She took the water and handed me the Scotch. "Drink, you lily-livered whelp!"

Her look terrified me. I took a mouthful. It burned my throat.

"Now I'm going to fuck you!" she growled.

She pushed me on my back, took me inside of her and began to pump with wild abandon. "Come, bitch!"

I came on her command. Holding myself for so long, under such intense stimulation, my orgasm was overpowering. My excitement was like an accelerant to hers. We shook in one another's embrace, feeling our bodies merge in a bright explosion.

Afterwards, I was lost in the warmth of her body. I felt playful and talkative. I wanted to hug and cuddle. I wanted her to laugh and express affection. But she was still irritated. She treated me coldly.

Certainly the intensity of our sex was beyond anything I had experienced. But did we have a rare thing *together*? Was she so jaded that she took such satisfaction for granted?

It occurred to me that perhaps her lack of sentiment and her abruptness were artifices to cover up the thrill she felt being with me. Surely the sense of privilege that was bred in her bones would not easily allow her to recognize the fact that she had fallen in love with her houseboy.

Such speculations sparked deep emotions in me. For a moment my feelings ran away with themselves. My conjectures fed my fantasies. I imagined that my Mistress loved me and that she was ashamed of this love, that her drinking was an attempt to drown her feelings. Alcohol enabled her to hide her warmth and affection behind a mask of coldness and cruelty.

Then, I thought, no. I was only a trivial pursuit for her, a cheap thrill. She knew I loved her. Toying with my feelings and playing her mean mind games were her most wicked pleasures.

She loved me; she loved me not. I could not tell which excited me more.

She pushed me away and took a swallow of Scotch.

"Bring me another cigarette," she snarled.

I brought the cigarette and lit it. She sat back against the pillows with her knees up and spread her legs. I lay with my head on the mattress looking up at the opening I so adored. As she smoked, she played with herself. I had a close look at her pretty pink insides. She had perfectly formed lips, rose-petal soft and dewy, and a most exquisite flame-red clitoris.

I told her how much I craved licking her puss.

"Puh-lease!" she said. "Your mouth is filthy and, besides, you are not very good at it."

"Teach me to be better. I will wash my mouth with soap if it makes you happy."

"Not now. Maybe some other day."

I felt so aroused. "May I lick your ass, then."

"Quiet! You're such a *guy*." She said the word with disgust.

She stubbed out the cigarette, again got on my back and began riding me. "I don't care if you get what you want or not," she said. "Anyway, I'm lazy. Why should I take the time and the trouble to teach you when I can satisfy myself like this." She continued rubbing herself on my back. As she became more excited she began to nip at my neck and shoulders. When I cried out, she flew into a fury, got off the bed and started rummaging in her closet.

She came back to the bed with a shoe that had a long, thick, square heel. She put the heel to my rectum, positioning the toe in the small of my back. Then she lay on top of the shoe and pushed the heel into me with the full force of her pelvis.

"Hmmm," she moaned, out of breath. "The little buckles tickle me. I feel the delicate straps on my clit."

I lay completely still. I dared not move for fear of being more painfully impaled on the heel than I already was.

"Whore! Pussy! Sissy!" she hissed. She reached around and grabbed my prick. "Come in my hand! I command you, bitch."

I did as I was told. But she was not finished yet. She continued jamming the square peg into the round hole. Now that my excitement abated, I began to feel the pain.

"I can fuck you any witchy way I want," she gloated.

"Of course, Madam."

"You're not some innocent boy."

"No, Madam, I'm not."

"You're bad for the things you make me do!"

"Yes, Madam, as you say!"

"And the lies you write about me! I should punish you severely."

She came to the height of her pleasure. She sighed and trembled.

She lay quietly for a moment, then she grew restless. She turned me over on my back and straddled my face.

Then I felt the hot stream hit my eye. She laughed and said I was her toilet. I begged her to stop but she peed in my mouth. She continued on my chest, then my abdomen, then my prick.

Relieving herself on me was a momentary fancy. When she was finished, she saw the mess she had made of her bed.

"Now look at what you made me do," she said, getting up and donning her robe. "Change the sheets. Quickly!"

She disappeared into her bath. I heard her running the shower.

I stripped the bed and brought the covers to the laundry. When she came back I was drying the damp spot on the mattress pad with a hair dryer I had found in the guest bath.

"Let me dry *you*," she said.

She took the appliance, turned it to high, and aimed it at my pubic area where I was still wet. She drew me close and pressed the dryer directly to my skin. Raising a few welts on my inner thighs brightened her mood.

She waited, sipping her drink, while I remade the bed. I turned back the covers and she slipped in and patted the place next to her.

"Sit here, boy," she said softly.

When I did so, she whispered in my ear, "Last night I had a dream that you and I were walking hand-in-hand through a fragrant garden."

I felt overjoyed that my Mistress dreamed such a thing. It was a tender vision for me, one that I would want to savor forever. But Lady Fair turned to Lady Foul. "Asshole! Do you really think such a dream was happy? It was a nightmare. You're just a fuckhead boy, and besides, the more I get to know you, the more I see how untrustworthy you are."

"I am the same every day. I feel the same and I do the same. I love you the same every minute."

"You're full of shit!" she hissed. "You're not good enough to serve me."

"No one is good enough for you, Madam," I replied. "But rest assured I love you and will always do my best."

She slapped me. "Lying whore! You say you love me so I won't send you back to your dull job at the grocery."

"No matter how you punish me," I said, "you'll never make me say I don't love you. I *do* love you."

"Do you love being treated as trifle?"

"I will accept anything to enjoy the pleasure of your company."

She slapped me again. I turned the other cheek. Indeed I was enthralled to be at the mercy of such a wild woman.

Without thinking, I blurted, "Perhaps if Madam admitted her love for me, she would feel less angry." I instantly apologized.

"What an arrogant mouse! Get out!" She pushed me from the bed. "Get the *fuck* out! I've had my sex for tonight."

The dismissal plunged me into a black abyss. I would have rather been whipped with Madam's meanest strap than discarded so heartlessly.

"Whatever you say, Madam," I said. "I'm sure you know best. I hope I have been of some small service."

She stared at me blankly. In her drunken state she did not even seem aware that she had told me to leave.

I bowed and made my exit.

On Sunday I woke up longing for her. When I brought her coffee, she was still asleep. I wished her a good morning. She sat up in bed without a nod or even a sneer. She went out of her way to show me that, even though she used me, she had no need of me, that essentially I didn't exist.

I went about my work cleaning the house. When she came down, I skulked off to another room, like a dog with his tail between his legs. I hoped she took notice of my submission and that such meekness was enough to allow me to continue to serve her.

Monday was the day she was supposed to render her decision. Overwrought with suspense, I brought her coffee as usual and lingered at her bedside.

"Why are you standing there?" she said nervously. "Don't you have something better to do?"

I had to remind her that I needed to tell Mrs Gooden whether I would be staying on at the boarding house.

"Oh, I'd forgotten," she yawned. "Well, I'm not in the

mood to think about you now. I've decided to give up cigarettes. I'm in a foul mood already. Come back later, will you?"

I waited an hour and returned to fetch her empty coffee cup and to see if she required anything. She was sitting at her vanity, plucking her eyebrows in the gilt-edged mirror. She picked up an eyeliner pencil and put the end in her mouth.

"I'm dying for a cigarette," she said.

She had me pull down my pants so she could suck me. I was highly aroused, but when she did not get the satisfaction she wanted, she turned her tweezers on me and pulled out several of my pubic hairs. Then she rubbed my left shoulder. The bruise had not fully healed. The skin was still raw and red. My whimpers of pain seemed to calm her down.

She bade me to stay while she put on her face. She looked at herself in the mirror with adoring eyes and said, "Boy, you still have much to learn, but you show improvement. You are acceptable."

I was so happy I fell on my knees and thanked her. I promised her she would not be sorry. Still looking in the mirror, she puckered her lips and applied another coat of lipstick.

My Mistress had a brownstone in New York City near the Park. I was thrilled and honored when, after the New Year, she brought me there. As in the country, I was to keep house, serve and run errands. She put me in a maid's room, a small cubicle on the first floor, off the kitchen. The door locked from the outside.

Her suite was on the third floor. It consisted of a spacious bedroom furnished with a Belle-Epoque bed, a mirrored dressing room and a white marble bath.

She had a roomy velvet-lined closet of ballgowns, cocktail dresses and dinner dresses. There were opera capes, blazers, overcoats, racks of dressy suits and endless shelves with gloves, shoes and handbags. There was a special section with temperature and humidity controls where she kept her furs. She kept her lingerie in a carved bureau, similar to the one at Lavender Hill. There was a metal safe built into the wall.

"I'm a good judge of character," she said. "You're a shallow piece of cock, full of yourself, but you're no thief."

She told me the combination and allowed me to look inside. She had platinum, gold, diamonds, pearls, jade and rubies, bold modern pieces and elegant antiques. Her treasures ranged in every style from simple to ornate. She was fond of snakes and dragons and collected bracelets, necklaces, pins and charms worked into their likenesses.

I was saddened to learn that she had a dinner date with James, a dancer for the city ballet. My anguish steadily increased until late the following morning when she returned. She saw my distress and took me in her arms. "I missed you," she whispered. She pushed me to the floor and took complete liberty with me.

She had no control of herself, yet she was in total control of me.

The lazy Queen wanted the royal treatment. I was privileged to help her make an art of wasting the day. I attended her in the bath, bringing her caviar and champagne, making sure the water stayed steaming hot and foamy. She rose sudsy and I rinsed her and refreshed her with cool water from the hand-sprayer. Then I dried her in luxurious cotton towels.

The mirrored walls in her dressing room created an infinite regress. After her bath she laid on the lounge there, looking at her reflections. My Mistress was the Hallowed One and I was her devotee. Both of us were madly in love with her. I went to my knees before her and looked at my lovely idol. I helped her paint her face and dress her hair. I buttered her skin with perfumed lotion. Permitted to speak, I was a feedback mechanism that echoed her thoughts. I extemporized a litany of my love for her, the Goddess of Beauty.

Overflowing with a vain, serene self-satisfaction only an enchantress in her prime time could know, she devoured me. As keeper of the Queen's penis, I felt totally one with her.

To be with her at her perfection brought me a joy that knew no bounds. Her exhilaration began to waver. Perhaps it was the thought that she would not be young forever and that someday she would cease to exist and all the worship in the world could not change the inevitable. Perhaps she simply became so full of herself she had no room in her heart for me. Or perhaps, having consumed me with her excessive and insatiable appetite, she had to regurgitate me. Whatever it was, she turned from beauty to beast.

She pushed me aside and told me to fetch her clothing. She was going to have dinner with James. As I helped her dress, my insides were tearing apart.

The Goddess was changeable as the moon. In February James was out, David was in. An actor with several small film credits and a large trust fund, David was a mainstay of the charity benefit scene. My Mistress got into the swing of social life. She went here, there and everywhere, having lunch, cocktails and dinner with different people.

For the social butterfly, the proper attire was most important. She still had me help her dress, but now, pressed for time, quite anxious about the image she projected, she was out of sorts and unreasonably demanding. In this phase, she felt no need to amuse herself with my adulation. Nevertheless, I remained with my insatiable, irrepressible need to be at her service. I did my best to function efficiently, but her wardrobe was complex. New clothes arrived daily. Once when I folded a blouse which she wanted hung, she stabbed me in the buttocks with a dragon stickpin.

In March she broke up with David. Instead of abating, her anxiety seemed to grow more acute. She smoked non-stop and drank far too much. It was impossible for me to anticipate what notion might cross her mind, what little drama might unfold. As best I could, I endured her ups and downs. When she said, "Jump!" I asked "How high?" When she said "Sit!" I asked "How low?"

In April we went to Lavender Hill. She had a plan to renovate some of the gardens which had become overgrown. She kept me busy all day. Sometimes she came out to watch me work. She would invariably accuse me of slacking off. That was her way to get me to work harder and faster.

Whenever she sensed a streak of resistance in me, she would attack it. The weather was inclement and I came down with a bad head cold. She saw my discomfort and sent me out in a freezing rain to plant a bed of primroses. After a while, she came out in her boots and slicker, under an umbrella, to check on me.

"Why is this taking so long?"

I stood up and defended myself rather hotly. "I'm working as diligently as possible but the rain and the sucking mud make this job impossible to do quickly!"

"How dare you raise your voice in your Mistress's presence!" She made me lie in the mud and used her boot to push my face into it.

Before she allowed me back in the house she had me kneel on the stone patio in my wet, filthy clothes. She turned on the hose faucet and sprayed me thoroughly clean with icy water. I shivered from the cold. She brought out a pen and a tablet of paper. She ordered me to sit at the patio table and write "I am a lazy mouse" three hundred times. An hour later when I handed her the wad of rain-soaked pages, she sent me back out to write "I will not shout in my Mistress's presence" also three hundred times.

I was being consumed piece by piece. Would she pick me apart thoroughly, break every bone of my spirit until there was nothing left to be vanquished, and then throw me away? Or was there no bottom? Would there always be another hard lesson for me to learn? Would it be a never-ending challenge for her to push me lower?

The summer was long and hot. She socialized less this year than last. After several false stops, she managed to give up cigarettes again and reduced her drinking to an occasional wine spritzer. She often walked the garden paths and sat meditating. I did my chores as silently and invisibly as possible.

Several times a week she would take me to her bed. Inside of her, I always felt the greatest happiness. I never missed an opportunity to tell her so. She seemed equally transported in the rapture of love. Sometimes she said she loved me. But after the act, if I continued to gush about my love, she was either indifferent or nasty.

Labor Day marked one year since I had come to Lavender Hill. My Mistress took me to bed with her. She was tender and I thought I detected some sentimentality in the way she held me. I felt warm and happy as I melted into her.

"Do you call that making love?" she asked.

"I'm sorry if you're not pleased —"

"Impudent beast! Don't talk back! You don't think I want to spend my life with you, do you? I want you out of my life! Out of my house! Now!"

She went to her closet, found the pillow case with my things and threw it on my lap.

The dismissal took me completely by surprise. I could not believe my ears. I did not want to believe them. The words were an agony for me.

I begged her to reconsider. "Please! I need you!"

"How dare you talk of your needs to me! That is the problem. You were here to satisfy me. You failed to do so."

"I don't know what to say."

She remained impassive. "Say, `Yes, Madam'," she sneered. "Then get your things and go."

Being separated from her was the worst punishment she could inflict on me and she did so capriciously. I could not choke back the tears. As I left, the hurt from all the poison I had swallowed welled up in me. I had a temper tantrum. I cried, screamed and threw things. When my Mistress saw me suffering so, she laughed. Here was a wretch whose happiness totally depended on her mercy. Hurting me was her ultimate pleasure.

I went back to Mrs Gooden's. Hurt terribly by the dismissal, I couldn't eat and I couldn't sleep. I lay in bed, crying and masturbating, thinking of my Mistress's cruelty. I wanted to die. However, the Goddess does not close a door without opening a window.

Norbury is a small town. The word got around that I was no longer in Burke Ketchener's service. There is a code among women of my Mistress's ilk that because a good piece of male meat was hard to find, he should not be left to waste. And, after all, one woman's impudent beast could be another's little angel. Burke was known for her meanness.

Her boy, having spent a year in a chamber of psychological horrors, would be easy pickings for any woman of more moderate demands.

"You have a call," Mrs Gooden informed me.

Elizabeth Spindler, a New York interior decorator who once visited with Mrs Eblis, was on the line. She asked if I would dine with her in the city. She said she had a proposition for me. She would not discuss anything further over the telephone.

The invitation kindled a will to live in me.

On the train, I felt a combination of deep loss for my Mistress and the apprehension of a virgin bride on her wedding night. My stomach fluttered with nerves. I thought I might throw up.

Ms Spindler was a well-groomed, self-assured woman. Her living space was quiet and luxurious. I complemented her on her design.

She said, "When I bought this apartment it was a wreck. But I have an eye for a bargain. I enjoy taking a neglected piece of property, fixing it up and selling it for a nice profit."

She offered me a seat on the couch.

"Did Burke allow you to drink?" she asked me.

"Occasionally."

"Would you like something?"

"I'll have whatever you do," I said.

"You needn't be so agreeable."

"White wine, then."

She handed me a glass of wine, poured herself a vodka and sat down next to me. While we engaged in pleasantries, she reached out and stroked my hair. I flinched.

"I know Burke punished you for no reason," she said. "You do not have to be so afraid of me."

"If you say so, Ma'am."

"Please," she said, "call me Elizabeth."

The wine began to take effect. I relaxed and welcomed her caresses.

"I understand your Mistress has a new *man*," she said.

The idea of my Mistress with another was like a dagger in my heart, but Elizabeth continued to stroke me and rip me apart by talking about my Mistress's current adventure with the French Ambassador.

"It must really hurt," she gloated as she fondled me. "You should be angry. You're a good boy and you've been mistreated. I'm going to heal you, but first I must break you further. Or do you not want to be free of the bond of pain that ties you to Burke?"

I shrugged. It was a hard question to answer.

"Well, then, how are you supporting yourself?" she asked.

"I have no job. My money will run out at the end of the month."

"Would you like to work for me?"

"What would I have to do?"

"I have many friends who can use a boy who knows his place. You would go where I tell you."

She did not wait for me to reply, but led me to her bedroom. She began to play with me again. She was gentle and soft. Used to my Mistress's cruel treatments, I was deflated in Elizabeth's arms. But Elizabeth did not seem to care. She pulled up her skirt and pushed me down. Her puss was fragrant and sweet. I used my tongue to please her. After she came, she patted my head and said, "Good boy. I'll get your prick working in good time. The important things are you're polite, you're clean, and you know that you're nothing in the presence of a woman."

Elizabeth took an interest in my writing. I gave her a few sample chapters of my love story. She said I had talent and encouraged me. She also thought it showed the proper attitude for a boy in my position. I was happy to hear her say so. She allowed me to be at my leisure until noon every day and I took full advantage of the opportunity to record more reflections on my life. When I wrote about my Mistress, I could feel her near me. I could smell her, savage and precious.

In the afternoons and evenings, I served in the kitchen, bath and bedroom. Elizabeth handled me roughly at times, but there were no beatings or harsh reprimands. She thanked me for my efforts and praised me when I had done well. She began to build a new confidence in me.

After a month she introduced me to a pale, undernourished, overanxious lady named Martine Chassis. I was surprised when Madame Chassis, a complete stranger, drew me close and kissed me. She smelled of gardenia perfume, Pernod and cigarette smoke.

I brought the women drinks. I heard Elizabeth tell Madame Chassis that I was available to her, if she was so inclined.

"You'll be pleased, I think," Elizabeth said. "He's very well-trained."

I was flustered by such a proposal. Madame Chassis took a sip of her Pernod, lit a cigarette, looked at me again and said, "Why not? I could use a little diversion and my maid's away. I'll try him for a week."

Elizabeth turned to me. "You heard," she said. "Don't be slow, boy. Obey. Go pack your bag."

Madame Chassis had a long car. She lived in Greenwich. I drove. She sat in the back seat, smoking and sipping Pernod from a bar she kept for the road.

She lived in a three-story Tudor mansion on a tree-lined street. It was mid-October. The Connecticut foliage was brilliant. We went inside the house and she showed me to a heavily decorated parlor. She lay on a long chaise upholstered with a zebra print fabric and ordered me to pour her a Pernod on the rocks. The bar was in a little nook in the corner of the room. When I returned with the drink, she had removed her skirt and was running her long, slim fingers inside her panties. She drank quickly and asked me to remove my trousers. Then she took my hand and drew me down. She was very excitable. She wasted no time getting on top of me. It was over in moment.

She lit a cigarette. "Elizabeth says that you're an honest and conscientious houseboy." She ran her finger across the top of the table by her side and made a trail through a layer of fine dust. "I had some construction done recently. My maid had to go back to Costa Rica because of a death in the family. I want you to clean."

I looked around. It was a lot of work. There were endless surfaces, rococo furniture, paintings with ornate frames, elaborate china lamps, knickknacks, figurines and sculptures. On one end was a glass cabinet filled with delicate objects, expensive pieces of glass and china. The cornices, moldings and decorative woodwork were richly detailed. I would have to crawl on my hands and knees to dust the baseboards and go up a tall ladder to reach the ceiling.

There had never been any commitment on my part or agreement of indenture to Elizabeth. I did not find Madame Chassis particularly appealing. It was plain that we had nothing in common. I wanted to leave. But I dared not. I was desperate for approval. I did not want to let Elizabeth down.

"I'll do my best," I told Madame Chassis.

"You had better not break anything," she said coldly.

I spent the remainder of the day mopping objects with a damp cloth and rubbing polish on the furniture. At six o'clock, Madame Chassis told me it was time to quit. She took me to a small bedroom with an adjoining bath.

"Clean yourself and come to my suite."

I did as I was told. Her bedroom was de luxe. On one side of the room the floor was elevated. There was a grand bed with frilly covers and a luxurious, velvet padded headboard. She was sitting on the bed, dressed in nothing but high heels and a frilly blouse. She took me without foreplay or ceremony, so fast it was hard for me to keep up with her.

Her thrill was over as quickly as it came. She lit a cigarette and said, "Make sure you look on the underside of the dining room table. I noticed some cobwebs there."

She had dinner plans with Niccolo. I fixed myself a sandwich and went to my room. I fell asleep early and woke at first light of dawn. I began in the dining room.

At mid-morning Madame Chassis came down, dressed in a lace nightgown. She said hello to me and asked if I wanted coffee.

"Yes, thank you."

"Well, come and earn it."

She drew me by the hand to the chaise in her parlor.

Madame Chassis availed herself of me when the inclination struck her. It was always over quickly. While I cleaned, she often swaggered around me, inspecting, drinking Pernod and smoking cigarettes. She had an eagle eye for details. Wanting to please her, I did a painstakingly careful and complete job.

At the end of a week Elizabeth came to have lunch with Madame Chassis. I cooked and served.

"I see what you mean about this boy. He's a pleasure to have around the house, always so obliging."

Elizabeth nodded to me, "Good boy!"

It felt good to be appreciated.

"How much did you say it was for the week?" asked Madame Chassis, taking her checkbook from her purse.

"Seven."

I drove Elizabeth back to the city. She chattered idly. She said she missed me and could hardly wait to get me to bed. I was stunned speechless by the exchange that had taken place between her and Madame Chassis.

We parked and went up to her apartment. She sat on the couch and patted the place next to her.

"You've been a good boy," she said and kissed me. "You should be proud of yourself. You earned seven thousand dollars this week. I hope you saved some love for me."

I accommodated her. Afterwards she took an envelope from her purse and said, "I've deducted my agent's fee and my expenses. Here is your share. Remember, you wouldn't get anything if I didn't have the contacts."

Elizabeth laid back with a satisfied smile. She picked up the telephone and dialed. I looked in the envelope. There were four one-hundred dollar bills.

"Deanna, darling. Elizabeth Spindler . . .Fine, fine. And you? . . . Glad to hear it. I have an interesting proposition. There's a boy here . . .Oh, you've heard? Yes, he's the one who belonged to Burke Ketchener . . .Care to have a look at him?"

Deanna Treadways came to lunch on occasion at Lavender Hill. She was a tall, blonde woman, aristocratic, somewhat brittle, with an aquiline nose. The way she looked at me made me fear she might be a poacher. I was in the kitchen making tea when she arrived. When I entered the parlor holding the tray, Elizabeth and she were standing, waiting for me. Mrs Treadways looked softly debonair in a cashmere top and tight stretch pants.

"Hello, Mrs Treadways," I said. "Perhaps you remember me?"

I bowed and Mrs Treadways buffed me in the nose with her purse. It did not hurt but it startled me. The dainty china cups and saucers and the silver coffee service shook, but I held steady and avoided disaster. The women laughed and sat on the couch.

"Of course," she said. "Burke's boy."

I put the tray down on the table. Elizabeth poured. Mrs Treadways helped herself to cream and sugar. "I spoke to Burke yesterday about him," she said to Elizabeth.

The mention of my Mistress made me tremble with longing. She knew that I was being passed around her circle. Why couldn't she be jealous?

"Burke said he was a dutiful boy," Mrs Treadways went on, "but impertinent. She grew tired of trying to train him."

"Oh, you know Burke," Elizabeth replied. "She can be dreadfully mean to the men in her life. What she calls impertinence is just a little boyish spirit. Overall, this boy keeps his inflated male ego where it belongs. Below his waist."

They laughed.

"Sit!" Mrs Treadways tested me. I went to the floor at her feet. She petted my head. "Good boy!" She pressed my face against her smooth muscular calves.

Elizabeth winked at me.

Mrs Treadways turned to Elizabeth and began chatting. She had rented out her estate in East Hampton and spent August in Europe.

"The fall is the best time in the Hamptons," she said. "I'm going to take a couple of weeks there."

She finished her tea, rose, kissed Elizabeth, turned to me and said. "Follow, boy! There'll be lots for you to do around the house and in the garden."

Elizabeth smiled and nodded.

I drove. Mrs Treadways sat in the back seat. She was very genteel in her manner. She kept her chin up and her eyes closed the whole way, listening to a recording of Liszt piano sonatas. The music was sad and beautiful, but it made me restless.

We arrived in East Hampton. She directed me down a narrow, wooded dead-end lane to a curving driveway, lined with stately copper beeches, blazing scarlet with the season, and gardens bright with purple asters and yellow dahlias. I took her to the house, an oversized stucco chateau.

She leaned forward, scratched the back of my neck, and said in a low growl, "I can't wait to sink my teeth into you." She pointed to a small rose-covered cottage behind the pool. "Wait for me in there."

I took my bag and walked across the lawn to the cottage. Inside, it was cozy, decorated with rose print fabrics, festooning drapes, a very English four-poster with curtains and a luxuriously upholstered headboard. I waited for Mrs Treadways on a fussy little couch.

I thought about my Mistress. How I missed her! I took out my notebook and wrote about how lost I felt.

When Mrs Treadways entered the cottage I rose. I did not know what to expect. There was nothing tender about the preliminaries. She went after me tooth and nail, nipping my neck and clawing my shoulders. I feared her. I could not tell how vicious she would get. But wishing to indulge her, I made sure my attempts to defend myself were unsuccessful and acted out all the apprehensions of a completely innocent boy being used roughly by a woman for the first time. I whimpered. My cries whet her appetite. She became wilder. She ripped off my clothing.

"I prefer boys with some spirit," she said with a scowl. "You're a dumb animal. You get what's coming to you." She boxed my ears, pulled me by my hair, and pushed me to the floor at the foot of the bed. She then sat on the bed and removed her pants.

"Come here," she said, pulling my head between her legs.

Her puss was moist, perfumed and lamb-soft. She began to pump. As her excitement mounted, she gouged my back with her talons.

After she came, she stretched out, glowing all over, and fell asleep, leaving me unsatisfied, kneeling at her feet. I slumped down, silent as a mouse, erect with excitement.

A half-hour later she opened her eyes and sat up. She looked at her watch.

"Get dressed," she told me. "I have an appointment for a massage in a half-hour. I'll show you what needs doing."

In the days that followed, Mrs Treadways had me weeding her gardens, scrubbing her floors, licking her from boot to buttocks. She disciplined me for no reason. Her favorite penalty was having me kneel on the brick patio while she sat on her padded lounge chair. If I fidgeted she would smack me across the shoulders with the rattan switch she used to swat flies. On one occasion the ache in my back and pain in my knees became so excruciating I began to cry. She took pity on me and called me up to lie with her on her soft pallet. We had intercourse several times and then she sent me back to the brick to kneel some more. The loss of such comfort added a new dimension to my suffering.

Mrs Treadways liked to play chess. In the evenings she would have me as her opponent. I was not a good player. Strategy had never been my forte. The considerable pain of having to kneel in front of the low chess table put me at an even greater disadvantage. One of her ploys was to have me play with a pair of her unlaundered panties on my head, arranged so that the crotch was directly over my nose and the silky lace filigree which trimmed her derriere was over my eyes. I was semi-blinded, semi-visible, driven to distraction by her mutton scent.

"The pony with the nosebag . . ." she taunted.

She checkmated me every game we played.

We also played Scrabble. I was more clever with words than she, but because I wanted to please her and because I wanted the game to be over fast, I chose to lose or at least play carelessly. She called me stupid and said I was no competition, but still took pleasure in winning.

During the first week in November the weather turned colder. Elizabeth arrived for lunch. After I served, I took my place, kneeling on Mrs Treadways' right.

"Preston is returning tomorrow," she told Elizabeth. "And while he likes boys, I don't think this one is quite his type. Anyway I've tired of him. He's *too* good. I like a boy with a little more fight in him."

"Bad boy! Come here!" Elizabeth said and stamped her foot. I went back to her on my hands and knees.

While Mrs Treadways wrote out her check, she said, "Do you know Helia Veaudor? I went shopping with her yesterday. She was complaining that she was bored. I happen to know that she likes her boys well broken-in. I would call her if I were you."

I left Mrs Treadways with Elizabeth. We headed west along the highway, past farm stands, antique stores and vineyards. We found Madame Veaudor in the parlor of her Southampton home. A woman nearing sixty, she was sitting on her sofa in a dressing gown, sipping champagne, smoothing her legs with scented body cream and watching a soap opera on television. Her face might have been pretty once, but the years had etched their lines and set her features in a stern no-nonsense frown. She did not have a good figure by conventional standards. But her pendulous breasts, paunchy belly and spreading hips and thighs appealed to my passion for decadence.

Elizabeth introduced me to her.

"I'm pleased to meet you, Madame." I bowed.

"Are you?" she said. "We'll see if you still say that after you get to know me."

She held out her hand for me to kiss. She had long, delicate fingers, neatly manicured.

"Turn," said Madame Veaudor.

I presented my buttocks. She grabbed me, digging in with her nails. "Yes," she said to Elizabeth, "I see how it could be amusing to have a slave for a while."

As if to seal the deal, the two women toasted one another with champagne and kissed. Madame Veaudor opened her lips and pressed her tongue into Elizabeth's mouth. I was surprised to see Elizabeth linger in the older woman's embrace.

"Call me if you have any problems with him," said Elizabeth, as she was leaving.

Madame Veaudor said she would be in touch.

When we were alone Madame Veaudor said, "Please disrobe."

By now I was used to strange women looking me over. As I dropped my pants, she went to a cabinet and removed a pair of surgical gloves. She put them on. The gloves were tight fitting and smooth as a second skin.

She bent me forwards and spread my cheeks. I stifled my sobs as she poked into me with her sharp fingernail.

Sometimes my Mistress finger-fucked me like this. She also sodomized me with the handle of her crop. Such intrusions were for variety and because my Mistress needed to claim her territory inside and out. I was supposed to be open to such encroachment, but I never was. My muscles involuntarily contracted.

"What a tight little bitch-boy you are!" said Madame Veaudor. "Have you still got your cherry?" She took a closer look. "I see Burke has you broken in, but she didn't do a very good job. Let me show you how we did it in a more romantic era." She took a handful of the body lotion, slavered it between my buttocks, and ordered me to push against her finger. She had an expert touch. I opened to it.

"There, my little asshole," she said, penetrating deeper, wiggling her finger inside me to make room for another. I squirmed and begged her to be gentle, but she was obviously intent on showing me who was boss.

Madame Veaudor was old but she was not slow. She knew exactly what she wanted. When she came, she gave a series of sharp thrusts, jerking me up and down as if I were a puppet on a stick. When she withdrew, I collapsed on the carpet in front of her, gasping with pain and pleasure.

"I understand you cook. I'd like to see what you can do."

Madame Veaudor led me to the kitchen. In the closet next to the pantry was a kitchen maid's dress. She ordered me to put it on. The black tunic had a heavy white cotton apron in front and ties around the back. Too small for me, it left my backside exposed.

She told me I would find a chicken in the refrigerator and the rest of the ingredients for *coq au vin* in the pantry. I am only a passable French chef. I did my best.

She dined alone at the long table in the dining room. She had me stand by while she ate. She was very critical. She pointed out every little thing that was amiss and even some things that weren't. I told her that I valued her criticism. I promised her I would become a better cook.

"I will correct your mistakes," she said, "and you will correct mine."

"Madame?"

"I understand you're a writer," she said.

"You flatter me, Madame."

"Well, I am trying my hand at it, too. I've always been a Tocqueville fan. Like him, I'm fascinated by America. I'd like you to proofread this for me. And, as an American, I value your comments."

She handed me a folder with a manuscript. "Go to your room and get started."

My room, just off the kitchen, was small but cozy. There was an adjoining bathroom with a sink, bowl, tub and bidet. The cabinet was equipped with an enema bag, tinctures of chamomile and peppermint and a perfumed lubricating jelly. After my initiation on the patio, I understood quite clearly the cleanliness that was expected of me.

I did not know what to expect from Madame Veaudor's manuscript. I settled into bed and began.

I find the disparity in America between the so-called intellectuals and the popular culture endlessly interesting. Personally, I think there is more to be learned about America by staying home and watching television than going to university dinner parties and hearing Ivy League Brahmins speak condescendingly of the "bourgeois culture" and how the ignorant masses are being steered by the media. These liberal academics think of the people as a comatose mob, brainwashed by commercial television. But, in fact, television is a window into the true democratic soul of America. The people vote with their viewing habits and all the hype in the world can't make a hit show. Yet the self-proclaimed cultural elite speak for the people without ever listening to them or getting to know the myths they live by. In fact, the humorless pedants who so extol the virtues of democracy are contemptuous of the actual tastes of the people . . .

Madame Veaudor wrote English as well as she spoke it. I found an unusually small number of typographical, spelling and grammatical errors. The following morning, when I brought her the corrected manuscript, she was sitting in the dining room wearing her night dress, having coffee.

"Well?"

"I found your impressions witty and engaging, Madame. And I couldn't agree more. You are a woman after my own heart."

This was not servile flattery. I was indeed affected by the things Madame Veaudor wrote. By no means was she a pretty woman, but she looked quite handsome to me now. I leaned over and kissed her. I felt myself opening, longing for her touch.

I spent the following days as Madame Veaudor's cook and the nights as her proofreader. While she was open to any suggestions I had regarding her style and allowed me a great deal of editorial license, she was a tyrant in the kitchen. She would walk around with an overbearing strut giving me instructions. Things had to be done her way and no other. If the food was not prepared to her exacting specifications, or if I left the slightest mess in the kitchen, she would call me a stupid asshole and poke me between the buttocks with the handle of a wooden spoon.

Her bedroom was formally decorated with eighteenth century antiques, including a bed with an embroidered gold fabric canopy and billowy curtains. In one corner there was a large television and, next to it, a gilt-edged escritoire on which sat a typewriter. She spent a good deal of time here, clicking away on the keyboard and watching the television at the same time. She changed channels frequently. She viewed everything, drama, sitcoms, game shows, sports, music, movies, news, with equal interest. Several times a day she would call me. I was wearing the scanty kitchen dress; she was wearing the gloves. I would bend forward, over the armrest of the red taffeta love seat, and she would take her fundamental approach, always seeking to make a little more space inside me for herself. At every new enlargement my unwilling muscles would tighten. If I complained, she would chide me.

"Don't flinch, asshole! Shut your mouth and open your other end wider!"

On the fifth day I graduated from manual forays to a chubby ivory dildo. She also used a long wax taper. It was a wicked tickle deep inside me. I obliged her as best I could, saying prayers to the Goddess that she would not penetrate too far.

With Madame Veaudor behind me, I improved in my culinary skill, enough for her to invite friends to dinner. Pierre Boyer and his new boyfriend, Clayton Rawls arrived one evening at eight. I expected she would have me wear a more conventional server's uniform, but she insisted I stay in my revealing kitchen dress.

Monsieur Boyer was Madame Veaudor's age. He was a fashion designer, an old queen with a haggard, pinched face. Clayton, a draftsman, was about my age, tall, thin and black. They were a good-humored couple. Monsieur Boyer seemed to sense my embarrassment. He complimented me on the way I was dressed. Clayton agreed it was quite becoming and praised Madame Veaudor for her daring sense of style.

I served duck with an orange sauce, pureed yams and haricot verts. Monsieur Boyer ate with relish and assured me everything about the preparation and presentation was excellent. I nodded to Madame Veaudor and said that I owed any success I had to her. She seemed pleased.

After dinner the three went into the parlor for cigars, brandy and conversation.

As always, when Madame began to offer her opinions about fashion, politics and art in America, I found myself wanting to be taken by her. Everyone noticed my swell as I refilled her snifter.

The conversation turned to sex. Monsieur Boyer told Clayton about the old days when he and Madame Veaudor both worked for Chanel in Paris. "We used to prowl the private clubs together," he said. "In one there was a trans-gender dominatrix named Dauphine who had a surgically-built clitoris. It was oversized for what it was supposed to be and she would use it to sodomize her slaves. Remember, Helia."

There was a moment of silence as Madame Veaudor puffed reflectively on her cigar. The memory of Dauphine made her eyes smolder.

"I once allowed myself to be Dauphine's victim for the evening," said Madame Veaudor. "Here's a little *coup d'amour* she showed me."

Madame Veaudor looked at me and patted the hassock on which she rested her feet. I knew what to do. I laid across it on my stomach, spread my legs and put my bottom up. Madame sat up and moved to the edge of her seat. I saw Monsieur Boyer put his hand in Clayton's lap and draw him close.

I felt Madame spill a few drops of brandy between my buttocks and place her cigar close to my skin. I felt the heat and smelled my delicate hair burning. I was paralyzed between pain and pleasure. Madame sensed when the thrill became unbearable for me. She drew back the cigar, puffed and allowed me a few moments to catch my breath. Then she spilled another few drops of brandy on me, and again began to singe my flesh. After a dozen rounds of this, the area around my hole was raw, blistered and exquisitely sensitized. I was ready for the taking.

Madame lifted her skirt, removed her underpants and placed them under my nose. The crotch piece smelled like *foie gras*. Then she got on top of me. She positioned her clitoris between my tender buttocks, pressed against my anus, and began to bump and grind against me, scratching my raw flesh with her pubic hair. Of course she did not penetrate very far, if at all. But the idea was there all the same.

She shuddered with pleasure, as did her guests. She was not going to allow me an ejaculation, but Monsieur Boyer interceded. Madame Veaudor placed her bare hand into my unlubricated crack and I squirmed before her with discomfort and glorious submission.

The following morning Madame Veaudor sent me back to Elizabeth on the train. Although there were plenty of seats, I stood the whole way. The burn on my backside was oozing and tender. As always Elizabeth was thrilled to see me. As always, when I had been with another woman, she inspected me closely. When she saw the burns on my buttocks and the tears in my anus, she gently applied a soothing, cool lotion, bringing me to climax with delicate strokes.

"Poor boy!" She kissed me. "You were sweet to indulge Madame Veaudor, but, in the future, you must remind customers that they are not to make marks on you or deface you in any way without consulting me."

She dialed the telephone.

"Hello, Helia? Elizabeth . . .Yes, I'm looking at the boy's backside . . .Yes, I'm sure you're sorry . . .Of course, it's perfectly normal for things to get out of hand, only I can't send him out like this . . .I'm glad you understand . . .Another three thousand should cover it. Yes, thank you . . .A pleasure doing business with you, Helia. Don't hesitate to call again. Bye."

Elizabeth let me stay in bed for three days. She cooked for me and applied the salve to my cuts and burns.

I never saw a cent of the additional three thousand.

Two days before Christmas, another woman came to Elizabeth's to meet me. The stranger was pretty, with thoughtful eyes and a kind mouth. I thought she wore more makeup than she needed. She had a good figure which she hid in a beige turtle neck and loose-fitting khakis. Her name was Judith Christian and she was a literary agent.

Judith was not like the others. She did not have me strip or see how quickly I would go to her feet. As it was late in the day, she invited me to have dinner with her. We sat in a noisy bistro and chatted. The topics ranged from music to politics to professional basketball to language. When I asked her about herself, she blushed.

"I've never done this sort of thing before, you know, hired a man," she explained. "But I'm going through a messy divorce. I need to heal, not get involved."

I assured her I would make no demands.

"I guess you're just what my therapist ordered," she said. "I've never had a slave. I don't think it is moral for one human being to own another."

"It isn't," I said. "And that's the fun of it. My pleasure is to love, honor and serve without expecting anything in return. You pay homage to what is divine in both of us by allowing me to do what I was born to do."

Intrigued, she raised her eyebrows. "You seem nothing like the men I've known," she said. "But I have not had much experience. My husband was the first man I was with and I was true to him. He was always a selfish son-of-bitch. Three weeks ago he announced that he was moving to Los Angeles to be with a woman with whom he's been having an affair all along." Judith's face changed. She became tense and tearful. "Even so, I still love him dearly. Do you know what it feels like to be betrayed by the one you love?"

I told her about my love for my Mistress. "When I was with her, whether she treated me kindly or not, the excitement was the same. Good feelings were mixed up with bad ones. Many times, I felt better when I felt worse."

"Yes, I understand that," she said. "But how do you feel now that she has cast you aside completely? Do you miss her?"

"I feel terrible and I miss her desperately," I said. "Nevertheless there is a piece of her in every women. When I serve others I feel I'm doing her will. And when I write, I find her inside of me."

"Elizabeth told me that you were a writer," Judith said. "She says you're pretty good."

"Elizabeth is being kind." I said.

"Some of the best writers think their work undeserving," she said. "When you feel you have something good, I'd like to see it."

Judith's apartment was on the West Side. Her bedroom was large, plainly furnished, and neat.

"I'm self-conscious about my body," she whispered nervously. "I need to see yours first."

I undressed and stood in front of her, pretending to be more embarrassed than I was. She ran her finger down my chest and over my belly, stopping just below my navel. Then she took me by the hand and put me under her bedcovers. She turned out the lamp, undressed with her back toward me and slid into the bed beside me. We lay close kissing. I told her I was hers to play with. If she wanted me to touch her, she need only say. Her hand went down gently. I felt her desire mount along with mine. But suddenly the glow of her pleasure was replaced by a pall. She slid out of the bed and went to sleep in the other bedroom.

Judith had a condominium in Miami Beach and invited me to spend the holiday week with her. We left the next day. The plane was delayed and we arrived late. Both of us were tired. Judith showed me to a small bedroom with an adjoining bath.

"Make your self comfortable." She kissed me on the cheek. "I'll see you in the morning."

I sunk into bed. I missed my Mistress.

The next day was Christmas Eve. I woke to brilliant sunshine. Judith invited me to breakfast on the beach. We sat in an outdoor cafe, basking in the warm sun, eating ripe mangoes and drinking fresh orange juice. Our conversation was lively. We passed the day together, talking, walking, sitting on the beach, and swimming in the warm, turquoise Atlantic.

At night the neon lit Ocean Drive. The restaurants were packed and festive for Christmas. Judith was a regular customer at *Le Soleil* and we had a table in a quiet, moonlit courtyard with a fountain and tall, stately palms. We ordered a bottle of champagne. Several times Judith cleared her throat as if she were about to speak and then apparently decided against it. I sat next to her in silence, sipping the champagne.

"My husband had reason for leaving me," she said, finally. "When we were first married, I made myself available to him, but I was never comfortable asserting my own needs. I never felt entitled. Soon sex became a chore for me. I didn't make him feel really wanted."

"Your pleasure is mine," I assured her. "Feel free to take whatever you need. But don't feel obliged."

"I see," she said. There was a lift in her voice.

After dinner, she suggested a stroll. There was a park by the ocean. The moon was full and the night was clear. Every frond had a silver lining. We walked across the sand to the shore line. We stood for a moment, watching the moon floating in the vast heavens, dancing like silver daylight on the foamy waves. She began to cry. Then she touched my hand. I turned to her. The ocean was reflected in her eyes. I held her close.

We went back to her condominium. The moonlight poured through the large windows of her bedroom. She sat on the edge of her bed and held out her foot. "My shoes —" she whispered, choking on the command. "Please."

I understood she wanted me to remove them. I went to my knees before her.

"Now my dress." Her voice rose with excitement. She stood and I loosened her belt and unzipped her. The dress fell to the floor. She stepped out of it and sat back down. She wore a plain white cotton bra and panties. I placed my head dutifully on her knee and pulled her panties down. She looked at me and looked at herself. She touched herself, parting her lips. Then she slithered forward, took my head between her thighs and pressed herself to my mouth. She tasted like roast pork and apple sauce.

"You are delicious!" I panted. I could feel her stiffening with excitement.

Her arousal slowly reached the point of no return. She squeezed my head tightly and twitched in an ecstacy that was a long time coming. She took me inside her and pumped lightly. My own climax contained none of the wild thrills I felt with my Mistress, but there was none of the pain, either. There was a different type of magic in the connection between Judith and me. As much as I missed my Mistress, I could not have felt happier at that moment.

We passed the week walking, talking, swimming, sun bathing, shopping, dining, and making love. Although she was an aggressive business woman, Judith had a gentle nature. She never exhibited the man-killer instinct of the sensual dominant. She did not make me feel low in her presence. Nor did I feel spontaneously submissive to her. I understood she craved comfort more than excitement. We spent New Year's Eve in the Jacuzzi, drinking champagne. She had plans to stay on in Miami. The following morning I was to fly back to New York. We went to bed early. Without her having to say, I understood. She wanted to lie close to me and nothing more.

She drove me to the airport. We thanked one another and promised to stay in touch, even though we both knew we would not.

I returned from Miami feeling rested and whole. I found Elizabeth a bit flustered. She told me that she had a special client coming that evening to consider me.

Special indeed! My heart skipped a beat when the client walked through the door. My Mistress looked more beautiful than ever. She greeted me indifferently. The peace I felt from my time with Judith was shattered.

"How are you and your friends enjoying my boy?" she asked Elizabeth as they sat down.

"It's your tough love that's made him so darling, Burke. You really do have the touch."

"I'm sure you've spoiled him rotten."

"I believe he's a person first and a piece of cock second, if that's what you mean. Have you come to take him back?"

"I can't decide," my Mistress said. "He is entertaining, but he's also such a nuisance, always underfoot. Ah," she sighed. She seemed out of breath. Was she becoming excited?

My heart yearned for her.

"I don't know what's come over me lately," she went on. "I'm feeling so wicked and he's such fun to torture. Only I don't know whether it will hurt him more if I leave him here with you or if I take him home and go rough on him. Would it be terribly inconvenient if I took him back?"

"Not at all. He's sweet and I'm very fond of him. But in this business, one can't get personally attached. And my customers like variety. Marilyn Michaels has a nineteen-year-old Laotian houseboy. Her husband will just not stand for it any longer. He is forcing her to discharge the boy. Marilyn can be quite temperamental. I'm sure she has this boy pussy-whipped to a pulp, just the type I like to use."

My Mistress turned to me.

"Yes, Madam."

"I'm going to Lavender Hill for the week to see about some renovations," she said. "Do you want to go with me?"

I wagged my tail. "You know I do, Madam."

"I won't be kind."

I wagged again. I understood.

"I will give you another try," she laughed. "I expect you to redeem your failings and your bad conduct."

My return to my Mistress's service was an unexpected as my departure from it. I waited in the hall while my Mistress wrote Elizabeth a check.

The drive to northern Connecticut took several hours. There were construction delays on the Interstate. As we crept along, my Mistress sat in the back seat, expressing her annoyance and blaming me for not taking the Parkway. As she squirmed impatiently in her seat, the car became suffused with her animal anxiety.

119

On several occasions, after long car rides, my Mistress would have me lick her backside to ease the fatigue of sitting. Would she grant me the privilege today?

Eventually we got beyond the delay. My heart beat faster with every passing mile. When we came up the winding country road to Lavender Hill, my mouth was watering and I was fully erect.

"My bags are in the trunk," she said coldly. "Bring them to my room."

When I arrived with her bags she was lying face down on her bed. Her bare bottom was up, beckoning.

"Come here!" she snapped.

I fell on her like a starving men. Away four months, I felt as if I had been away forever; I felt as if I had never left.

It was January, with icy rain and snow. While my Mistress met with an architect, contractors and decorators about re-doing her bedroom suite, she had me work outside, clipping branches and raking.

In case there were any doubts about to whom I belonged, when we returned to New York, my Mistress invited Elizabeth and her friends for tea. She had me wearing nothing but a pair of her black lace panties. The evidence of my enormous feeling for her was plain. I served Madame Chassis, Mrs Treadways, and Madame Veaudor. I was grateful that Judith was not present to see me subject to such indignity.

The modern pagan queen held court with a terrible majesty. I stood by while she told her guests the story of how she used her craft to pursue and maintain sexual power and opportunity.

"I remember the day I got my first period," she said. "My Aunt Faith told me it was curse, a sign from God that women were born to suffer. She told me that I was weaker than boys and that I must be careful not to be overpowered by them. I was fortunate to have my Aunt Brittany set me straight at a young age. A long-legged misanthrope, Aunt Brittany taught me the edge I had over the opposite sex. But I think I would have come to this realization anyway. My common sense — or was it my woman's intuition? — told me that while nature gave boys size, she gave women an attractive appearance and a craft for wearing false faces.

"When I was fourteen, I had many older boys pursuing me. Although my Aunt Faith forbid me to date, I would often go out, using the ploy that I was visiting a girlfriend. My tactic was to seduce the boy before he seduced me. For the first part of the evening, I laid on the feminine charm. I flattered my escort about his looks, his interests, his mind, his body, his clothes, his accomplishments and abilities. On the surface I seemed soft, sweet and adoring, but inside I was full of contempt for my victim and his vanity.

"Later, after the movie and the food, I would brazenly ask if we could drive somewhere. When we parked, I immediately took the upper hand. I only let the boy touch me if he was really, really hot, and then only briefly, to tease him. My fun was making him want me more than I wanted him. Sometimes, if I felt like it, I would go all the way. I swallowed my boyfriends between my legs, but in my heart I was untouchable. Most of the time I used any trick, any lie, any excuse, to abruptly end the make-out session. If the boy persisted, I told him my aunt was going to Europe tomorrow and we could have a whole week of fun in my house. The false-promise worked every time. The boy would take me home. When he called the next day, I would say I was busy. If he continued to annoy me, I told him the truth: that he was noisy, or smelly or loathsomely clumsy. The ends justified the means. And I could be pretty mean. The mating dance was a call to arms in the battle of the sexes, a war game I felt compelled to win.

"In college, I continued my conquests. I had many suitors begging for my favor. Most of them were rich older men who thought they were God's gift to the world. They wanted to project themselves as knights in shining armor. I saw through their ironclad exteriors. Their self-confidence was a mask for their needs and insecurities. They were unable to control the vagaries of their hormones. I ignored — actually, I reversed — all moral precedents for sexual relations. These customs were set by men, men who would use any strategy to seduce women. I used every lure to engage the man. I would flirt and flaunt my charms; I would be nonchalant; I would be secretive and mysterious. The more deceitful I was, the higher the man seemed to regard me. I encouraged the man to pursue me; then I frustrated him, and in the end betrayed him. That gave me a sense of my true power.

"I married Dario for thrills. It was good that he died, for we surely would have killed one another. For all the glamor of being married to Barton, I wasn't happy. I pursued my affairs without concerns for morality, appropriateness or discretion. He disapproved of my independence. I was willful and could not be stopped from plotting my own way in the world. Finally, after much provocation, he divorced me. Since then I've handled my intrigues however they best suited me."

Seven years passed. I cooked. I cleaned. I worked in the garden. I ran errands. I served in her bed when she was in the mood. I saw dozens of men come into my Mistress's life and leave it. She would keep her lovers until they professed their lifelong devotion or became confounded by her sporting behavior. Then bored or put-out, she would send them away and start over with someone new.

She knew I suffered when she was with other men. I was trained not to show it, although often enough I broke down in front of her. She would laugh. The demonstration of my unhappiness gave her pleasure.

I never entertained thoughts of other women. My Mistress was the only woman for me, and I told her so constantly. I prided myself in being a loyal, devoted servant.

One summer afternoon I was serving my Mistress tea on the patio when Mrs Featherstone paid a surprise visit. A stiff woman, with ivory skin, pale blue eyes and a serene smile, Mrs Featherstone was president of the Boston Arts Council, an organization that helps support struggling painters and sculptors. When several of the grantees went out of their way to turn public opinion against BAC by desecrating conventional religious images in their art, the council lost its municipal funding.

"Burke darling, next Friday there's an auction to benefit the Council," Mrs Featherstone told my Mistress. "I'm here to ask you for a contribution. Do you have anything we might sell to raise money?"

My Mistress looked around. Her shameless eyes landed on me. "I'm going to Paris next week," she said. "I won't be needing my boy. The right lady or gentleman should pay well for seven days with a well-disciplined slave."

My heart broke. She would not allow me the self-respect I felt being hers and hers alone.

"As always, darling," said Mrs Featherstone, "you are generous to a fault."

Mrs Featherstone thought my Mistress's idea was so clever that she decided to donate her boy Scott. Together my Mistress and Mrs Featherstone called Mrs Trilling and Mrs Harrod and convinced them to lend their boys to this little adventure.

On the day of the auction, I took the train to Boston. I arrived at Mrs Featherstone's town house on Beacon Hill in the late afternoon, an hour before the pre-auction inspection. Mrs Trilling lived in Boston. Her boy was already there, helping set up chairs. Mrs Trilling, like my Mistress, insisted her boy be nameless. Scott attended to the refreshments.

Mrs Harrod appeared with Prince. I was happy to see my old friend. Although we were forbidden to speak, I understood from his cheerful nod that he was equally happy to see me.

Mrs Featherstone decided to bind us together for effect. She sent Scott to the hardware store for some chain and padlocks.

Chained wrist-to-wrist, stripped to our underclothes, the four of us stood on the block at the pre-auction inspection. I had Scott on my right and Prince on my left. I wore a card pinned to my briefs. It read,

> Seven days with a trained boy at your complete disposal. Bidding will start at two thousand. Boy courtesy of Burke Ketchener.

Penrod Lawton, a prissy designer, showed great interest in us. He was horribly grabby. I shuddered to think what he might be like in private. Then there was an old crone named Mrs Hines who smelled of mothballs and cat food. When she patted my behind, I thought I might be sick. I prayed to the Goddess that there be a kind soul at the auction to outbid these two filthy lechers. The thought of being sold to either Lawton or Mrs Hines alarmed my fellow slaves, too. We huddled together in fear and loathing.

The bidding started at seven o'clock. Mrs Featherstone acted as the auctioneer. Item One was dinner for two at

Emilio's. It went for one hundred and seventy-five dollars. Item Two was a Shaker chair donated by Miss Thorndyke. The high bid was seventeen hundred dollars. Mrs Trilling's boy was Item Three. Lawton took him for four thousand, Mrs Hines stole Scott, Item Four, for twenty-five hundred. When I came up, Lawton bid twenty-five; Mrs Hines three; Lawton thirty-five; Mrs Hines four; Lawton forty-five.

"I have forty-five hundred," said Mrs Featherstone, "do I hear more?"

She did not.

"Going once, going twice . . ."

I closed my eyes trying to steel myself for the worst.

"Five thousand!"

It was a woman with a haughty false-British accent.

"I have five thousand from Mrs Radcliffe-Browne."

At lunch I had heard my Mistress and her friends speak cattily of the wife of the art dealer Oscar Radcliffe-Browne. They said she was a plain woman who fancied herself a great beauty, a commoner who put on airs and an uninspired decorator who overcharged her customers. She had the deplorable nerve to snub my Mistress and Mrs Harrod by not bothering to respond to their dinner invitations.

I opened my eyes. The new high bidder, whatever her flaws, did not look as bad as Penrod Lawton or Mrs Hines. Mrs Radcliffe-Browne had short blonde hair, a large nose and was overdressed in a red silk evening gown and red high-heels studded with rhinestones.

"Do I hear five-five, Mister Lawton?" Mrs Featherstone asked.

The old queen made a sign that he would pass.

"Going once, going twice? Burke Ketchener's boy is sold to Mrs Radcliffe-Browne for five thousand."

Mrs Radcliffe-Browne also made the top bid for Prince.

Mrs Radcliffe-Browne took Prince and me from the auction still chained together and in our shorts. The Radcliffe-Brownes lived in a four-story brownstone in the Back Bay Area. It was about nine-thirty when we arrived. Mrs Radcliffe-Browne drove around back and beeped her horn. The maid, a young blonde woman in a starchy black and white linen uniform, came out. She looked to be about twenty-five. Her name was Caroline. She laughed when she saw what her mistress had in the back seat of her car. Mrs Radcliffe-Browne told Caroline to bring us to her study on the second floor. She would be with us shortly. Caroline marched us into the house by the back door while Mrs Radcliffe-Browne went around to the front.

The house was furnished with fine antiques. There were fresh flowers everywhere.

Caroline took us up one flight to Mrs Radcliffe-Browne's apartment. It was decorated with gilt-edged mirrors and faux-finish gold paint. Before she left us, Caroline reached up under her skirt and felt herself. Very saucy for a simple New England girl, she waved her wet fingers under our noses and poked them in our mouths. She tasted sweet, like creamy clam chowder.

Mrs Radcliffe-Browne swaggered in soon after. Prince and I stood stiffly, side-by-side at attention. She walked in circles around us. Having us fettered and at her command increased her scorn. She played with our private parts. She had an exciting touch. She led us to an adjoining bedroom and had us go to our knees facing one another. She pulled up her gown. She was not wearing panties. She slipped between us and stood in her rhinestone heels while Prince licked her ass and I slavered her vagina. She was sopping soft and smelled like fresh ham and lavender perfume. After she came she pulled my head back by my hair and sprayed a salty, sweet juice in my face.

Still in her red dress, she lay on the bed and took a moment to catch her breath.

"Here, boys." She clapped.

Prince and I lay on either side of her. I was on her right. I kissed her right cheek and rubbed against her right thigh. Prince did the same on her left. Our hands, chained together, caressed her belly and below.

She pulled me directly on top of her and slid me inside her. Her left hand toyed idly with Prince. She moaned with excitement. Then, after I came, she pushed me aside and took Prince, while she teased me. Then she took me again. She seemed as if she wanted to go on all night. But there was a knock on the door. Caroline informed Mrs Radcliffe-Browne that her husband had arrived.

Mrs Radcliffe-Browne ordered us up, back to attention. She then rose, straightened her clothing, combed her hair and left the room. She was back in five minutes accompanied by a chubby older man with round, ruddy cheeks and an indulgent smirk. He looked like Bacchus.

"Aren't they adorable!" Mrs Radcliffe-Browne said to him as she unchained us.

Prince turned to me and gave me a look of dismay. The Radcliffe-Brownes, like so many of their arty ilk, were a decadent couple.

"Like two peas in a pod," Mrs Radcliffe-Browne went on, patting Prince and me on our bare bottoms. "I don't need them both. Take your pick, Oscar dear."

Mister Radcliffe-Browne hovered over Prince.

"Have you been to Thailand?" Mister Radcliffe-Browne asked him.

"No, Sir."

"Well, you're going. To keep me company."

"Yes, Sir."

"Good. I like a cooperative young man. Come. I'll need you to pack my bags."

Looking anxious, Prince went with Mister Radcliffe-Browne. I was left alone with Mrs Radcliffe-Browne. She took me by the hand, back to her bed.

"When bedtime comes, Oscar and I go our own ways," she said matter-of-factly. "Once upon a time I had a lover. Then I had a breast removed because of cancer." She turned her back to me and asked me to help with the zipper on her dress. She slid out of it and unhooked her bra. Her left breast was perfect. To its right was a scar. "After this happened, my lover never touched me again. *You* have no choice. Come here."

I spent the night in her bed. She went after me as if she had been starving for attention. I did my best to fill her insatiable appetite. I found her passion contagious and I performed time and again. But she outlasted me. When she could squeeze no more juice from me, she turned on her side, curled into the fetal position and pushed me down, placing my head, facing her, between her inner thighs. She rocked herself to sleep pressing her vagina on my face and spent the night pumping gently, sighing in her sleep with pleasure.

Spending the night with my nose up her puss, I did not get much sleep. In the morning, she took me inside her and squeezed a little more out of me. She rose refreshed, ready to go, and dismissed me. Exhausted and famished, I went to the guest bath to freshen up. All I had to wear was my shorts. I went to the kitche, anyway.

Caroline informed me that Mister Radcliffe-Browne and Prince had already left for the airport. She insisted I make and serve the Mrs breakfast. When Mrs Radcliffe-Browne came down, she was dressed in a tweedy three-piece suit. She sat in the dining room. I brought her tray with orange juice, tea and cereal.

She ate in silence, reading the newspaper, and departed promptly at nine-thirty for her design studio. I was left under the supervision of Caroline. She sat in the dining room, in the place vacated by Mrs Radcliffe-Browne, and ordered me to bring her a cup of coffee, then get busy clearing the breakfast mess. Soon Antoinette, the maid from the house next door, arrived. She was a heavy-set mulatto from New Orleans with straight hair and smoky eyes. It greatly amused Caroline to have me to boss around. Even more, she enjoyed showing off in front of Antoinette. Caroline ordered me to remove my shorts. I obeyed. The two girls taunted me. They cruelly threatened to splash hot coffee on my naked body. I understood that their threats were in fun, but I trembled nonetheless.

Caroline showed me the house. I saw Mister Radcliffe-Browne's apartment. While his wife's rooms were furnished with rare antiques, his had every deluxe modern convenience. Seeing his bed with its rumpled bed covers made me wonder how my friend Prince was faring. Caroline led me through a spacious drawing room to the guest quarters and, finally, to her room.

"Start in here," she said, the words rolling off her tongue as if she was to the manor born. "Put my things away, make the bed and clean the bath. Then do the same upstairs."

While I did the housework, Caroline sat in the dining room eating pastries and drinking coffee with Antoinette.

At eleven Antoinette left and Caroline came to inspect my work. The Mister and Mrs apartments passed, but her room did not. She slapped me for leaving dust on her bedside table. She had me remake her bed with ironed linens and scrub her toilet until I could see my face in the bowl.

It passed the second inspection.

She made me kneel. She lifted her skirt and dropped her panties. Her vagina had pendulous, fleshy lips. Her clitoris stood out like a ripe raspberry. She grabbed me by the ears and pulled me to her. She had not recently washed and smelled as unappetizing as yesterday's chowder. When I recoiled she slapped me and held me by my hair. I licked her, rolled her clitoris gently between my lips and sucked until she came. She made me stand, covered with her clammy juice, and tickled me with a feather duster. Just as I was about to explode, she looked at her watch and said, "Hmm. Twelve-thirty. The Mrs is very precise in her habits. She always returns for lunch at precisely one. She doesn't like to wait. Put on your shorts and get to the kitchen! She's having a Caesar salad — she likes extra anchovies in the dressing — and grilled salmon."

I felt filthy. I wanted to wash my hands and face but Caroline forbid it.

I prepared lunch and Mrs Radcliffe-Browne arrived punctually at one, as Caroline said she would. Mrs Radcliffe-Browne insisted I stand by while she had her lunch. She ate the salad, took one bite of the salmon and left the rest. I had not eaten since the evening before. I wanted that fish, but I did not dare ask.

"Clear this away," she said. "Tell Caroline to give this salmon to the cat and come back with my coffee."

When Mrs Radcliffe-Browne finished her coffee, she took me upstairs. I helped her remove her jacket, trousers, stockings and panties and then accompanied her to her bath. She sat on the pot and urinated. She ordered me to clean her with my tongue. Her pee was sweet. Her vagina smelled pleasantly musty, most welcome after Caroline's. Then she rinsed my mouth with mouthwash and had me lick her ass while she brushed and flossed her teeth. She stood me up, pushed me against the wall and took me standing. It was over in a flash. She attended herself at the bidet, dressed, putting on fresh stockings and panties, combed her hair, fixed her makeup and left, all without saying a word to me.

Soon after Mrs Radcliffe-Browne was gone, Antoinette returned. Caroline had more salmon. She had me prepare it and serve it to them in the dining room. I had to stand by while they ate. I thought I would faint from hunger.

The door bell rang.

"That's Inga!" said Caroline to Antoinette. "Mrs Trilling's maid. I invited her to lunch." Caroline turned to me and pulled off my shorts. "Go, boy. Get the door."

I was self-conscious about my lack of clothing. I checked through the peephole to make sure it was indeed Inga and not the postman. I saw a buxom blonde in a maid's uniform. She was holding an oversize purse. I opened the door and bowed. Inga burst into laughter when she saw me.

"This way, Ma'am," I said, trying to preserve some dignity, and led her to the dining room.

Inga followed, very rudely poking my bare bottom.

Caroline ordered me to set a place for Inga and serve her. Inga happened to have a magnum of fine champagne that she had taken from Mrs Trilling's cellar. The three maids lingered for an hour, drinking and eating. The content of their conversation was essentially no different from their mistresses'. They gossiped and talked about sex. They criticized their lovers and talked with contempt about men's perversions. The main difference was that the maids' choice of words was considerably more vulgar than their mistresses', especially as the alcohol took effect. They called me "Fuckhead", "Asswipe", "Dicknose" and "Cuntsucker". Unlike their bosses, they ate every bit of food on their plates.

When I took away their plates there was nothing left except a few pieces of salmon skin. I battled to maintain my reserve, but my empty stomach got the best of my intentions. "I spent last night exhausting myself servicing the Mrs," I said, "and now have spent the morning working hard for you, all without a single bite to eat. I'm hungry."

"Oh fuck!" said Caroline with an affected sympathy. "We forgot to leave Pussyface food."

They laughed.

"I'll fucking give you something to eat," said Caroline. "Kneel." She pointed to the floor at her feet.

I went to my knees. She pulled up her skirt. Her fat vagina was open, swollen and glossy wet. She made a crude joke about seafood, grabbed my hair and pulled my nose into her nasty nether mouth. When she got what she wanted, she invited Antoinette and Inga to do the same. Inga had her period. Her puss was bloody, but sweet. Antoinette had a sweaty smell. She pulled my hair so hard I cried.

The three maids laughed. Having served them all, I begged for real food. They agreed I had earned it.

Caroline went into the kitchen, opened another tin of anchovies and put them in a bowl on the floor in front of me.

"Here, Pussyface."

I ate like an animal, licking the fishy oil from the sides of the bowl, my cheeks and chin.

Although I begged to be allowed to wash my face and brush my teeth, Caroline would not let me. I cleaned the kitchen and the parlor while she passed the afternoon playing cards with her friends. The maids knew Mrs Radcliffe-Brown would return promptly at five-thirty. At five the card game broke up. Caroline ordered me to kneel and satisfy sweaty Antoinette one last time. Then I had to lick Inga's bloody hole. After they left, at the last minute before Mrs Radcliffe-Browne returned, Caroline ordered me to suck her.

I imagined Mrs Radcliffe-Browne would want me clean and well-groomed when she came home. At the least, I did not think she would want to find me sweaty from work and drenched in the beastly secretions of three servile women.

However, when Mrs Radcliffe-Browne saw me, she smirked. She could tell what debasement her maid had put me through, but found my pitiable condition humorous and, yes, exciting. She led me into her bedroom. Once more she prevailed on me to service her. The feeling of being unclean overwhelmed me. When I could not provide the amusement she sought, I pled with her to be patient with me. She was deaf to my appeal. She went into her closet and came back with a rod made from a trio of strong, green birch twigs tied together. It was a fitting instrument for a stern Yankee mistress.

She led me to a wooden bench and ordered me to lie on my belly. For form's sake and to increase her amusement, I showed reluctance. She threw me down roughly and tied me hand and foot to the legs of the bench. She put a pillow under me to raise my buttocks.

I took ten lashes stoically. She mounted me, sitting on my savaged buttocks like a rider on a horse. I felt her dainty spray. All at once the feeling welled up in me. I wet the pillow.

Every day Mrs Radcliffe-Browne wanted more from me than I had. Every day Caroline teased and goaded me. She fouled me continually. I was glad when the seventh day arrived.

Mister Radcliffe-Browne and Prince returned from Thailand. Prince, in contrast to the look of alarm on his face when I had last seen him, now seemed relaxed, cheerful and comfortable in the company of Mister Radcliffe-Browne. I was in a tormented melancholy.

Prince and I took the train together back to Connecticut. He told me that he was only called upon briefly to minister to Mister Radcliffe-Browne. The rest of the time Mister Radcliffe Browne hired girls and would watch Prince engage them in a variety of unusual acts.

"As it turned out," he said, "I had a great time."

When I saw my Mistress again, I fell trembling to my knees and kissed her boots. I told her how much I missed her.

She kicked me away.

"You filthy whore!" she shouted.

She did not look at me or touch me for three months.

I passed my thirteenth autumn at Lavender Hill. The warm weather turned chilly. The green leaves changed to red and gold. At the end of October, the trees were almost bare. Halloween morning was gloomy. The skies were gray and the air was cold. When I served my Mistress her coffee she told me to bring the car around at noon. We were going for a ride. She would not say where.

A few minutes past noon, she appeared in a full-length cape, high boots and long leather gloves. She had me bring down a garment bag, a small piece of luggage and a package from a costume shop in Manhattan.

I asked her if I should have packed for overnight. She told me not to ask questions, just drive.

We took Old River Road north. She sat quietly, looking through the window at the little towns in western Massachusetts. The houses were decorated with jack o' lanterns, skeletons and ghosties, sheets suspended from the naked trees. Everywhere along the roadside were large, colorful piles of leaves being swept up in the autumn wind.

As we crossed into Vermont, the wind picked up and the temperature dropped. The bare trees looked ominous. We exited the state highway and took a back road that meandered north. We went through several very small towns. Again, all the homes were decorated for Halloween. At a town called Providence Gorge, we turned onto a winding, narrow, unpaved road. We drove for miles through a naked forest of birch and maple.

In the twilight we came to a driveway with an iron gate and a sign that said VV. There was a television camera. My Mistress lowered her window to identify herself. The iron gates opened. We drove on a series of hairpin curves to the top of the mountain. There stood a house of monumental proportions made of stone block and huge timbers. As we walked to the entrance, we paused briefly to admire a full moon over the gorge in the east. It looked like a fat pocked-faced pumpkin peaking at us through a break in the threatening clouds. The scene, mysterious and desolate, inspired a romantic feeling in me. I turned to my Mistress and told her I loved her. She looked at me with glittering, wet eyes, but said nothing.

There was a brass wolf's head on the door. It's lower jaw, on a hinge, was the knocker. Underneath was a small brass plate which read

COUNTESS VLADIMIRA VALANESCU.

My skin prickled. I had heard my Mistress tell Mrs Harrod about Countess Valanescu. She was a Rumanian noblewoman. Before the Second World War, as a young woman in the old country, the Countess would take boys from the village to her castle. My Mistress whispered when she told Mrs Harrod that the Countess had a penchant for blood sport and other unspeakable things. I was finally going to meet the legendary cockatrice.

We were greeted by a dour, middle-aged blonde woman wearing a suit and tie. She introduced herself as Madame Ursulak, the Countess's assistant. She welcomed my Mistress graciously, looked me over coldly and invited us in.

The house was furnished with antiques, oriental rugs and heavy drapery. It was very dark. I peeked into the dining room. The long, wide table was set with candles, crystal, linen and china. I counted thirteen places. Madame Ursulak showed us to a parlor with a glowing fireplace. Over the mantle there was a reproduction of a Paleolithic painting showing a man wearing a jackal mask and stag's antlers. My Mistress sat on a leather couch by the fire. She told me I was to remain standing by the door.

Madame Ursulak excused herself and went to get the Countess. In a few moments a tall, slender, bloodless woman entered the parlor. She was wearing a flowing robe of black satin with sable cuffs and collar. I expected the Countess to be in her late seventies at the very least. While she was gaunt and looked tired, as if she had just gotten out of bed without enough sleep, she looked no older than sixty. Behind her she was pulling a boy on a leash. He was on all fours and moving fast to keep up with her. He was naked except for a leather collar. He had a gold ring in his nose and another on his penis. When he passed me, I saw his back and buttocks were marked with what seemed to be bite marks. The boldness of it made me shudder.

I could see from my Mistress's expression that she had genuine reverence for the older woman. The Countess sat next to my Mistress and embraced her. The boy lay with his belly across the Countess's feet as if to warm them.

The Countess looked at me. The lines around her mouth set in a diabolic frown. "Is this It?" she asked.

"Yes," said my Mistress. "He's made a passable slave, but I can go just so far training him. He'll need some professional finishing if I am to make him my pet."

When I heard my Mistress say *pet*, my heart sang. She had plans that would raise my position in her life.

"You've come to the right place," said the Countess. "You American women are too soft. A fine companion animal must be dehumanized. To train it, you need an Old

136

World attitude. Of course, your boy will have to stay with me for a while. Will you want a 'loaner'?"

My Mistress nodded slyly. The Countess passed my Mistress the leash handle. "This is Thing," she said, raising her foot. "Thing! Crawl!" She snapped her fingers.

The boy slid on his belly like a snake to my Mistress's feet.

"Thing has been with me a month. He no longer has any concept of being human. He's as gentle and accepting as a lamb. You'll see what improvements I hope to make in your boy."

My Mistress petted Thing and pulled on the penis ring. She poked his swag with her boot-toe. Thing showed no signs of either fear or pain, but was fully compliant. I was dismayed.

The Countess turned to me. "Remove your clothing." Her voice was stone cold.

I felt exceedingly uncomfortable, but I did as I was told.

"Kneel!" she said, pointing to a spot on the middle of the floor before the fire.

Eager to please, I did so. She held me by the hair and looked up at the painting. "Horned One, I bring you a new servant."

A maid entered with two large crystal tumblers full of brownish-red liquid.

"Vodka and beef bouillon," said the Countess, taking her seat again. "It's my afternoon pick-me-up."

The maid was dark-haired, dark-skinned and had a hollow look in her eyes. She, too, wore a leather collar. From the way her black silk tunic clung to her, it was obvious she had no underclothing. I could see the outlines of metal rings in her nipples.

"Stay, Ivana!" ordered the Countess.

Ivana stood in place next to the Countess.

My Mistress and the Countess drank and laughed.

I understood from the conversation that there was to be a Halloween party. "As I told you on the phone," Countess Vladimira said, "this little costume dinner for the Sabbath is a tradition of mine. Guests must come dressed as the opposite sex. To make it interesting, I try to get an even mix of singles and couples, straights, gays and lesbians."

As my Mistress listened, she pulled Thing's nose ring and placed his head on her lap.

"Dinner will be at ten," the Countess went on. "At midnight, a servant who has been made into dessert will be laid on the table. The guests will then have their treat.

"Sweet one, will you be our treat again this year?" The Countess reached out and caressed Ivana's shoulder.

Ivana blanched.

A devilish grin spread on my Mistress's face. "Let's have my boy prepared also."

"So it shall be, darling," said the Countess. "Now, you must be tired after your ride. If you will follow me, I will show you to your room."

"Come, Thing," my Mistress tugged on the leash handle.

My Mistress left with the Countess, followed by Thing. Ivana and I remained in the parlor.

She knelt next to me and whispered, "I dread this night. Last year I was put on the table covered with mocha cream, chocolate mousse and cherry syrup. The guests all had a lot of wine and were feeling full of mischief. One of the gentlemen, done up like Marie Antoinette, bit my breast so hard I still have the marks." She pulled down her dress and showed me.

I asked her about the body rings.

"The Countess demands unflinching loyalty from her trainees," Ivana whispered ruefully. "She has hundreds of ways to break you."

I wanted to find out more details about what might be in store for me when Madame Ursulak appeared in the room with the kitchen help, six strapping Rumanian women dressed in white aprons.

Madame Ursulak pointed to Ivana and said, "Chocolate man," then pointed to me and said, "Chocolate woman."

Two of the women led Ivana and me into a bathroom with a large shower. I was already naked. They stripped Ivana, removed her collar and had us lather and rinse ourselves thoroughly in very hot water. Then they shaved us from head to toe. I mourned the loss of my head hair. I shrunk as their razors whisked away my pubes. Ivana endured the same with stoic resignation. The women were very professional about it, careful and sure of themselves. Neither of us received a nick.

They washed us and rinsed us again in hot water, so hot I nearly had to scream.

In the kitchen the other four women were preparing for us, melting long bars of chocolate in big stainless steel pots. They mummy-wrapped us in long bands of warm sticky taffy. As the taffy cooled we became fixed with our arms at our sides and our legs spread slightly apart. They lifted us onto long silver platters. They gave me enormous breasts of thick caramel cream and used large strawberries for my nipples. They poured a thick layer of warm chocolate over my genitals and made a pocket in it while the chocolate was still soft. When it cooled and hardened, they filled the pocket with raspberry jelly and liqueur. Then they enclosed this syrupy goo in another layer of chocolate which they molded to look like a vagina.

Ivana was given a large erect penis made of nougat with a center of caramel cream. They made her testicles out of jelly candy. They put bitter almonds on our eyes, candied cherries on our lips, marshmallows in our ears, marzipan on our hands and feet, and poured the raspberry liquor all over our throats and abdomens.

They placed plastic straws in our noses so we could breathe. Then both us were encased from head to toe in a thick layer of melted chocolate. We cooled just in time for dessert. Like pall bearers the six big women lifted us on our trays one at a time and brought us to the table.

I could not see. The riotous applause and laughter were muffled by the marshmallows. Then I felt teeth ripping at my chocolate shell, tongues searching for what the coating concealed. Most of the munching was on my "vagina". I was terrified that someone might bite too hard and damage the reality underneath, but I dared not move lest my nervousness bring about the very thing I feared. Still, frightened as I was, I could not stop rising with excitement. There were sighs of delight and amused laughter as my prick broke through the taffy. I could feel the liqueur running down my thighs. All mouths went to my midsection, licking and biting to get at the viscous trickle.

After the guests had their fill, Ivana and I were sent with Madame Ursulak to wash off the remains of the chocolate and other confections.

When I was clean and dry, Madame Ursulak buckled a leather collar, similar to the one worn by Ivana and Thing, around my neck. The leather was new and very stiff. It was tight; it almost choked me. Any movement of my head, up, down or to the side, caused painful chafing on my neck and throat.

She then attached a leash to the collar and pulled me back to the parlor. Hundreds of candles were lit in ornate candelabras; their light was reflected in the mirrored walls. Everyone was in costume. Men dressed as women, women men, were lounging about, drinking. My Mistress, wearing a Prussian army general's uniform, was sprawled on a couch. Thing was on his hands and knees before her.

Countess Vladimira sat on a high-back chair sipping a clear drink from a crystal chalice. Although she still had a haggard, pale countenance, the night and the flickering candles became her. Dressed in a black tie and tails, she looked distinguished and quite handsome.

Madame Ursulak brought me to the Countess.

"Sit!" she commanded.

Shaking, I took my place by the Countess's wing-tip shoes.

My Mistress glanced at me and gave me a pitiless smile. She began teasing Thing. She pulled him by a chain attached to the ring in his nose to sniff her puss and then, as he began to warm to her, smacked him across the nose with the leash handle to drive him back. Although he whimpered at the strokes and jerked uncomfortably in his constraints, he came back tamely for another sniff when she offered it, knowing full well the swat that would follow. The pain I felt watching her sport added not only to her pleasure, but to her beauty as well. In the rosy glow of her excitement, my Mistress was divinely captivating. I longed to be at her mercy.

At midnight, Ivana brought the Countess a flute. A capable musician, she played a solemn air. Her tone was dark and smooth. The guests joined arms and formed a circle, men and women alternating. With their eyes closed, they danced slowly around the center of the room. As the procession ended, the guests took to kissing and caressing one another with good cheer.

The Countess put down the flute and pulled me to her on the leash. She put her goblet to my lips. It was straight vodka.

"Drink, my little lambkin! It will relax you." Her voice was soothing, seductive.

She made me drink until nothing was left. It did relax me. Madame Ursulak brought another crystal goblet of vodka, this with a long, thin gold swizzle and several gold rings at the bottom. The Countess rose from her seat to lean over me. Suddenly, the hugging and laughter ceased. The guests went back to their seats. All eyes were on the Countess and me.

The Countess removed the stirrer and held it up for me to see. It was, in fact, a golden needle with a sharp point. I recoiled at the sight of it. From what I understood, the Countess was capable of any cruelty.

Vladimira's eyes gleamed. She licked her lips. I could see her long teeth. I could smell the evil on her breath. There was heavy breathing of expectation from the guests. My faith in the Goddess wavered. I began to grovel.

"In the name of Jesus, Ma'am, don't do whatever it is you plan."

"Ssshhhh!" the Countess hissed. "Be still. There is no escaping this. Lie back. If you fight, you might hurt yourself."

I looked around the room, hoping someone would sympathize with my predicament. But my terror was part of the show. All eyes were glazed with pleasure, my Mistress's especially. I closed my eyes and lay on my back, face up, praying to whatever higher power would listen that this Lady be kind.

I felt the Countess's cold bony fingers pull back my nostrils and rub vodka on the cartilage between them. "This will only hurt a bit," she said. "But don't move. If you do, I can't be responsible."

Then — oh! — with a quick jab she pierced a hole between my nostrils. She quickly inserted one of the rings from the bottom of the glass and gave it a little pull. I felt my flesh stretch at the flick of her finger. Blood ran on my upper lip. The Countess bent down and kissed me, lapping my blood with her tongue.

I sobbed and shook. My breath came fast and my heart beat wildly, as she began kneading my left nipple and rubbing vodka on it. I knew what was coming. I steeled myself and I prayed. With the same fast motion she pierced me again and inserted the second ring. She sucked the blood that ran down my chest. She did the same with my right nipple.

She was sure and quick with the needle, as if she had performed these procedures thousands of times before. For a moment I lost my fear and began to trust her. Then she poured vodka on my plums and took me by a loose fold of skin. My fruit shriveled in response to the danger; the pits sought shelter in my pelvis.

"No!" I cried. My teeth chattered. My spine tingled.

She warned me to stop trembling.

I felt the jab, like a lightning bolt from the All-Powerful. My right sac had a gold ring in it. She pricked again. The same fate befell the left. She knelt between my legs and bent forward. I felt her tongue curl around the blood.

Then I felt her lips on mine. Her kiss was soft, smooth and warm. Her breath was sweet. I opened my eyes. The Countess seemed to have undergone a remarkable transformation. Her skin was firm and pink. The cruel lines on her face were gone. Her hair was raven black. Her eyes were wide and entrancing.

Had feeding on me rejuvenated her? As a woman in the prime of her life, the Countess was more horrifying than she was when she was an old hag. She was the devil and my Mistress was in league with her.

Madame Ursulak brought five gold chains, each of them several feet long with a tiny latch on one end and a finger ring on the other. She handed them to the Countess who clipped the clasp ends to the rings on my body and put the finger rings on her left hand. She demonstrated how, with the slightest movement of her fingers, she could jerk me this way or that. I was defenseless, terrified to think of what she could do on a whim.

She could also make me stay fast when my every involuntary muscle wanted to move. She tightened the slack in the chains, detached the leash, and gave me several swats across the back with it. The blows hurt, but I dared not even twitch or flinch for fear of tearing my skin where the rings were attached.

There was a round of applause from the company. They appreciated the skillful way that the Countess had turned me into a human puppet.

The drinking continued and the party got livelier. Madame Ursulak brought out a quartet of the Countess's other trainees, two males and two females, to dispense as favors to the guests. The males wore frilly nightgowns; the females boys' briefs and tee shirts. Madame Ursulak invited the guests to explore the old mansion. She said they would find more of the Countess's trainees, ready for the taking, tucked in here and there. Trick or treat. Several guests slithered off to investigate.

I spent the remainder of the evening on my knees at the Countess's feet, looking mournfully at my Mistress who continued to tease Thing.

A man dressed as a belly dancer and a woman dressed in sheik's clothing sat on the love seat next to the Countess. The three engaged in a tedious conversation about the medicinal properties of night-blooming flowers. It had been a long, exhausting day. I felt sapped. I wanted to sleep. Whenever the Countess felt my head sink to the floor, she moved her hand and I had to adjust my position.

In the gray light before dawn, the party broke up. Dinner guests kissed the Countess goodbye and left. House guests threw dice to see who would bed down with which trainee. I was left with Vladimira. Once again she looked fatigued, gaunt and gray as the morning. Her cheeks fell into wrinkled jowls. Her eyelids drooped. I shivered apprehensively as she led me by the chains in my body rings to her bedroom. Her movements seemed to become stiffer with each step.

Like the rest of the house, her bedroom was sumptuously furnished with hulking antiques, plush carpets, tapestries and red velvet drapes. The bed was a four-poster. The fine linens and fur blankets were turned back. The lace-embroidered pillows were plump. It all beckoned, a sight for tired eyes.

The Countess sat on the edge of the bed and used the chains to yank me to my knees in front of her. She spent a few moments playing with me, frightening me by waving her hand and stretching my flesh, making me hop quickly to or fro.

She pulled me forward, turned me face down and kissed me on the left shoulder where I still bore the evidence of my Mistress's first blow in the form of a red mark, a bloodstain tatoo the size of a radish. I felt the Countess's teeth break my skin. As she licked the wound, she became aroused. In the spasms of her pleasure, she once again seemed to become young and beautiful.

I helped her remove her shoes and trousers. Her male costume was complete down to the pinstriped boxer shorts. I helped her remove these, too.

She had a shock of thick black hair and a plump vulva. She had a smell that was both musty and fresh, like rain in the woods. Her lower lips, warm and moist, beckoned to be kissed. But when my lips touched them — swat! — the leash came down across my nose. Bait and Batter, it was the same game that my Mistress was playing with Thing. The Countess had me by the plums. I had no choice but to kneel still while she buffeted my face. Then she drew me to her again. As I neared her puss and became wild for it, she struck me with all the force her bony arm could muster.

The game obviously excited the Countess. As she became more animated, she became bloodthirsty once again. I shook in pain as she nipped at my shoulder.

I thought vampires were mythical monsters. Even in my wildest fantasies I never entertained such gruesomeness.

When the Countess had her fill of me, she took the rings from her hand and, using a small padlock, attached them to a metal rod in the frame at the foot of the bed. She pulled a cord and Ivana came in. I watched as the maid helped the Countess into an elaborate black lace bedgown.

The Countess then had Ivana lie down next to her. The two kissed and fondled one another. Ivana left and the Countess fell asleep lying on her back. With her bony hands folded across her navel and her spindly, goose-fleshed legs motionless, she looked like a corpse. I was filled with repulsion.

I tried to get comfortable. The rug was soft enough, but the chains were too short for me to lie flat on the floor. With my buttocks on my heels and my upper body bent forward, I could not sleep more than a few minutes at a time.

At noon Madame Ursulak entered the room with some bouillon for the Countess.

The Countess was slow to wake. She groaned. Without opening her eyes, she said she was very tired and planned to stay in bed for the remainder of the day. "Take Vermin away," she pointed to me, rolled over and went back to sleep.

Madame Ursulak unclasped the chains from my body rings, attached the leash to my collar and pulled me down the hall, down the back stairs and outside to a large grassy area with some flower gardens planted with asters and ornamental cabbage.

It was November 1. The Vermont hills were bare. The air was chilly, the sky overcast. I was naked. Madame Ursulak led me to a wooded area and stood over me, watching contemptuously as, shivering with the cold, I answered nature's call. On the way back to the house, we stopped by a stream. I was allowed to wash.

We entered the house by another door. Madame Ursulak's suite had a large bath, a sparely furnished bedroom and a large office where she attended the Countess's business interests. There was an old English desk, several telephones and a computer. In one corner of the room was an antique circus cage made of sinuous iron bars. Beside it was a long couch with a leopard-skin print fabric on which a black poodle bitch was asleep.

The dog, who seemed unusually large, was elegantly groomed and as svelte as an animal could be. She wore a jeweled collar. She woke and barked to greet us.

"Cleopatra is very playful," said Madame Ursulak. "Come, Princess. Say hello to the new boy."

Cleopatra jumped up and pranced toward me. She put her paws on my chest and began to lick my face with great enthusiasm. I am not particularly fond of dogs, but I stroked her head to be polite. Rather than calm her, my touches seemed to inflame her affection for me. She was very strong. She pushed her wet nose into my crotch and no matter how I tried to move her head aside she would not budge. I looked to Madame Ursulak, hoping she would intervene, but she stood by watching with a wide smirk, as if she enjoyed the difficulty I was having coping with the animal's inordinate fondness.

"Fetch, Princess," Madame Ursulak said. Before I could fight her off, Cleopatra took my prick in her mouth. Evidently the dog was trained for this little sport. She softened her sharp teeth with her long tongue and her furry lips. Although she was quite gentle, I held my breath, quailed and pleaded that this game had gone far enough.

"You must learn to trust your trainers," Madame Ursulak replied sternly. "You have nothing to fear from Cleo. Poodles are the finest hunting dogs. They can take the most delicate game bird to their Mistress without so much as ruffling a feather."

It was a lot to take on faith, but I dared not say so.

"Here, Cleo!"

The dog minced her steps gracefully as she brought me to Madame Ursulak.

"Good girl!" said Madame Ursulak, giving the dog a kiss and a meat biscuit.

Relieved to be in human hands, I instantly became erect.

"Down, boy." Madame Ursulak pushed me back to my knees.

"He's all yours, Cleo," she said.

The dog came at me again. Before I could raise a finger in my own defense, Cleopatra pushed me on my back and wiggled her wet hindquarters over my naked loins. I heard Madame Ursulak laughing. I tried to push her off but she remained planted, eagerly sniffing me, licking my face. While I struggled, Cleopatra shook her nappy coat with pleasure.

Madame Ursulak unleashed me, pushed me into the cage and locked the door. It was a tight space; there was barely room enough for me to sit. I had to curl up.

While Madame Ursulak worked, fatigue overwhelmed me. I began to doze. This was not allowed. She poked me with a cane and woke me up. Overtired, I became very restless and began to stir. She poked me again and told me to be still. She had a letter opener that was razor sharp. She told me that if I didn't settle down she would cut off my ear and feed it to the dog.

This threat quashed any further fidgeting, although it made me considerably more restless inside.

At two in the afternoon, my Mistress entered the office. I prayed she had decided to take me home.

She looked at me in the cage and laughed. "Boy," she said, "you're going to stay with Countess Valanescu for a while. You must do exactly as she and Madame Ursulak say. Don't you dare make me ashamed of you."

"Please, Madam, no! Don't leave me!"

"Quiet!" My Mistress snapped and turned to Madame Ursulak. "Darling, if he steps out of line, you have my permission to do whatever it takes to knock him back in."

I cried when I saw my Mistress depart. My stay in hell had only begun. I sat in the corner of the cage and brooded. At three, Ivana brought Madame Ursulak's lunch, a veal chop, salad and a glass of red wine. I felt very hungry. I begged for something to eat.

Madame Ursulak jabbed me and told me to be silent. "Countess's orders," she said coldly, "you are not allowed food during the day."

While my mouth watered, Madame Ursulak ate indifferently. She nibbled on the salad and gave the meat to Cleopatra.

While she drank her wine, she offered me water by placing the mouth of a bottle between the bars. Then she began teasing me, walking around the cage, reaching in here and there, one time nudging me, another time caressing me. In that closed space, I could not turn fast enough to see where her next gambit was coming from. Her legs were thin and fit easily between the bars. She lifted her skirt, moved her panties aside, took one of the iron poles between her lips and rubbed herself against it. She ordered me to lick the wet metal. I slavered the bar and extended my tongue to get to her, but she moved away and hit my nose with the leash.

I implored her to allow me to ejaculate, but she forbid it. She said it was time I learned to take teasing like the dog I was. Then she turned and left the office. I spent the remainder of the afternoon and the early part of the evening locked in, alone. At least I was finally able to get some sleep.

It was dark when Madame Ursulak woke me. I felt leaden-brained and disoriented. She took me out of the cage, attached the leash to my collar and led me. Having gone all day without a bite of food, I was starving. My senses were sharpened by deprivation. The smell of roasted poultry permeating the house made my mouth water. We entered the dining hall. The Countess was sitting at the head of the table, having dinner with several friends. She looked tired, but seemed to liven up when Madame Ursulak brought me to her feet. Cleopatra, sitting nearby, wagged her tail when she saw me. The guests murmured, eager for some diversion.

The Countess took a grape from the table and waved it under my nose. It was like forbidden fruit.

"Lie down!"

I obeyed and she gave me the grape. I was rewarded similarly for rolling over and sitting up.

Next she took a slice of duck breast and waved it in front of me. The meat had an irresistible smell. I opened my mouth to take it, but she held it back.

"Indulge the Princess." She pointed to Cleopatra. The dog, having been through this before, was lying on her back. She had her hind legs spread and was wiggling her tail eagerly.

I refused.

The Countess waved the juicy scrap under my nose again and gave it to the dog. Watching Cleopatra wolf it down, I felt famished, so weak I realized that I could only hold out for so long. It was only a matter of time before I would do whatever it took to get some food.

I spent my days caged or led about on a leash by Madame Ursulak. Gradually, the leather collar stretched and became more comfortable. I grew accustomed to the limits the chains and rings imposed on me. I took my vulnerability as a matter of course. At night I did tricks for scraps at the Countess's dinner table. I even got used to the debasing acts I was forced to perform and the sinister things that were done to me.

Vladimira made love with her teeth. Did she really change from a bony old crone to a voluptuous beauty by taking sustenance in my blood, or was this all in my imagination? After all, I was starving and deprived of sleep. I could have been delirious, unable to tell the difference between dreams and reality.

Late one night, after I had been with the Countess for what I judged to be two weeks, Madame Ursulak joined the Countess in her bedroom. I lay still in my chains while the Countess used a strip of sharp paper to make small incisions on my finger tips. She invited Madame Ursulak, a vampire in the making, to suck. The Countess also cut me behind my ear and drank from there. Both of them were greatly stimulated by their draughts.

Whether it was something she tasted in my blood or my bovine acceptance of its letting, I don't know, but, licking her lips, the Countess declared me trained. My Mistress was to pick me up the following day. Until then I was under

Madame Ursulak's supervision. She put me in the cage and teased me by fingering her puss in front of me.

She left the office but said she would be back. I was deeply weary and stimulated at the same time. I was tempted to ejaculate but I was frightened of what Madame Ursulak would do if she came back and caught me. The iron bars left me nowhere to hide. I was trying to sleep when Madame Ursulak returned. She was dragging Ivana on a thick brass chain.

"No, I don't want this," she pleaded.

"The Countess demands it," Madame Ursulak said resolutely as she unlocked the cage and pushed Ivana in with me. "Do your best, bitch."

Madame Ursulak told me that Ivana was ovulating and the Countess wanted her pregnant. I was to do it. The space was very small. Ivana was all over me. An abject slave, twitching with anxiety, she was unable to draw the line between her fear of pregnancy and her sexual arousal. I felt compassion for the poor girl but I also felt her wet puss in my lap. Already pricked up from Madame Ursulak's teasing, I could not keep myself from penetrating Ivana. The first coupling was over in a flash. Prodded by Madame Ursulak's cane and Ivana's averse attraction, I came in her seven times before dawn.

At noon the following day Madame Ursulak, leading me on a leash by the collar, presented me to my Mistress.

"Sit!" Madame Ursulak ordered me.

I instantly fell to the floor at my Mistress's feet, wagging my tail. Madame Ursulak passed the leash handle to my Mistress. When I felt that familiar hand pull me, I thanked the Goddess.

"Heel!" I went to her heel.

I was something less than human. My Mistress pulled on each of the rings that the Countess had installed in me.

"Now when you get out of line, I'll just pull here . . . or here . . . or here . . ."

I jumped. My Mistress gave a spunky smile. I could tell when she was aroused. I was thrilled to be going home.

She took me to New York. In my absence she had hired Julia, an impenetrable, straight-faced Peruvian who spoke little English. My Mistress insisted I wear my collar and my rings at all times. I was thoroughly embarrassed in front of Julia. However curious the maid might have found me, she showed no reaction. She made it clear that what we did was none of her business.

Julia was staying in the room by the kitchen. My place was upstairs in my Mistress's boudoir. I hoped one day to be my Mistress's pet, and now that I got my wish I could not tell whether it was an upgrade or a step down. Often it was a more difficult and thankless position than being her slave. As her slave I had prescribed chores. I could gain satisfaction and a measure of self-esteem by doing the tasks set before me to the best of my ability, regardless of whether my Mistress appreciated me or not. Now she treated me as if I were a dumb animal. I was not permitted to write. Where once I felt I had value, not only as a servant but as a writer, now, as her pet, the companion of my Mistress's idleness, spoiled one minute and target for her perverse whims the next, I felt completely worthless.

Still, it did not take long for me to become habituated to the luxuries and the thrill of being so much in my Mistress's presence, even if, in my subhuman position, I rarely had her undivided attention. I did not want to go back to cooking, cleaning and running errands. It was cold outside. I lay at her feet by the fire as she made her calls, read her mail and her magazines or watched television. She performed her bath and beauty rituals, fingered herself and even went to the toilet as if I weren't there.

Lying at her feet, I was in a continual state of arousal. She liked to have me erect, consumed with desire for her. If she noticed me flagging she would tease me by rubbing my swag with the toe of her shoe or letting me sniff her vagina. Being near her night and day, the tension that built up in me became overpowering, but she did not take me inside her any more often. I would rub myself against the floor, begging her to tolerate my need. At first she indulged me, letting me roll on a cashmere throw, but when Julia reported that the dry cleaner could not remove the stains I made, she forbid me this much-needed release until she had a need of her own, or, if she was feeling indulgent, she would take me with her into her water closet. While she sat on the commode, I lay belly down and squirmed on the cold tile where I wouldn't leave a stain. She would call Julia to mop up after me. The solid woman went about her work without expression. It might have been a spot of spilled milk for all she cared.

As a concession to practicality, I was allowed to use a toilet. Several times a day, my Mistress would walk me down the hall to the guest bath.

My Mistress kept my food bowl in the foyer leading to her water closet. She fed me only once a day, a small amount of wheat pilaf that Julia bought at the gourmet deli. I ate either directly from the bowl or used my hands. It was delicious but not very filling. I was always so hungry that I wolfed it down in no time. Once in a while I got treats, a can of tuna, a small piece of cheese, a chocolate bar or, if I begged hard enough, scraps from her plate. On Thanksgiving, she gave a dinner party. I stayed locked in her bedroom, chained to her bed rail by my body rings. When the party was over she took me down. Mrs Eblis was having coffee in the kitchen. To demonstrate to her friend my total domestication, my Mistress had me eat a slice of turkey breast directly from the splattered kitchen floor. Meanwhile Julia was making soup from the turkey carcass. She stepped around me without batting an eyelash.

My Mistress also pampered me. Once a week, she scrubbed me clean in a big soapy bath. Then she powdered me and perfumed me. She sat on the love seat and patted the cushion next to her.

"Up, boy," she said.

I leaped up. She brought my head down and put my nose into her lap. She petted me.

My Mistress did not dispense pleasure without pain. During some of these heavy petting sessions, she would make a small cut on my shoulder with a razor and suck my blood. At my next feeding, she would pierce her pinky toe with a hat pin and let a few drops of her blood run onto my food. I figured this sharing of our plasma to be a bewitching ritual which secured a domestic familiar as an extension of its owner.

My hair, shaved by the Countess's confectioners, had grown back. My Mistress liked my head shaggy in front and tied in a pony tail down my neck. She used it to pull me about. But she thought my body was too woolly for the fondling minion of a suave woman such as herself. Wearing a magnificent full-length mink coat given her by one of her admirers, my Mistress took me to Monsieur Bari's, the Madison Avenue salon she frequented. She rarely took me out on the street. I was thankful for that. Not everyone had the blind eye that Julia had. I wore a scarf to hide my collar, but I felt humbled when passers-by noticed my nose ring. I was thoroughly mortified at the salon. I was the only male customer on the premises — and with body rings and dog collar no less. Monsieur Bari, Barry Zimmer, that was, and his assistant Miss Kim were totally professional.

"I just adore body-piercing," said Barry with rapturous excitement, holding his palms to his cheeks. "Isn't he magnificent, Miss Kim?"

Miss Kim agreed. I was magnificent. She could sense my embarrassment. She told me she had worked in Greenwich Village. She had seen it all.

Their good cheer put me at ease. My Mistress asked them to wax my legs, chest and buttocks. I had had my share of rough treatment. The waxing was a pleasure by comparison. My Mistress vacillated about whether to have my pubic fleece removed and finally, at Miss Kim's suggestion, settled on a bikini wax. I was also manicured and pedicured and I received the latest skin treatments.

Manhattan's Upper East Side is home to the world's most overindulged animals. On the way home, my Mistress stopped in a fancy pet shop. She insisted that I try on a heavy rhinestone-studded velvet collar to replace the leather one. The salesgirl who attended us was astonished. She could not keep from laughing as my Mistress turned me head this way and that to see who the collar fit. I gagged on my embarrassment. My Mistress maintained an aloof smirk. My Mistress also brought me into a lingerie boutique and bought me lace panties and cashmere briefs in large sizes and dark colors that matched her bedroom decor.

Sleek, spoiled glamor boy, I lay by the fire transformed from mouse to pussy.

In February, she began a fling with a man named Eric. I ate my heart out when I heard her coo to him on the telephone. Twice a week, she stayed at his apartment. On one chilly morning she came in and found me lying on the floor in her bedroom, crying from boredom and feeling myself go to waste. She used the warm spot between my legs as a muff to warm her toes. The teasing became too much for me. She ordered me to stop, but I, poor pup, lost control and wet the rug.

"Bad boy!" She acted as if she were furious. She rubbed my nose in the sticky little puddle. Then she beat me with her slipper, heedless of my whimpers for mercy.

She went out with Mrs Eblis. I felt furious, angry that she treated me with such disregard. At the same time, how I longed for her! I saw her slipper on the floor, the one she spanked me with. I had to be bad. I took it in my mouth and began to chew, thrilling to whatever punishment she would inflict when she discovered my transgression.

As I existed solely for the amusement of my Mistress, I was to remain continent until she released me. It was natural for me, when my Mistress went out, to spend my unrequited passion. She knew of these breaches, but most of the time she chose to wink at them. She took pleasure in my failings. They proved I was a weak, pitiful, lowly animal who couldn't help himself. But sometimes, inconsistently, there was reproof and punishment. Beating me only made it worse.

On one occasion, after she gave me a stern lecture and sound spanking, she came home early and caught me red-handed, as it were.

My Mistress shook her head. She said that I was ill and insisted I see her psychiatrist.

For my first session my Mistress accompanied me. Doctor Karla von Sturm was a trim woman in her mid-forties who wore a tight blouse, leather pants and thick-rimmed glasses. She had a serious, bored expression and spoke through clenched teeth in an affected prep school accent. My Mistress ordered me to lay on the couch. She sat in an armchair next to the doctor.

"I don't know what I'm going to do with this little pup," my Mistress said. "He can't keep his paws off himself. He makes a mess on the floor and he chews up my slippers."

The doctor questioned me carefully about my childhood and my sexual experiences and fantasies. I told her that I had a relatively happy, uncoerced upbringing. I did not feel I was the victim of traumatic abuse. Although my life was by no means conventional, as far as I could see my experiences were well-integrated with my fantasies.

"For all the pain," I said, "being with my Mistress is my fondest dream come true. I love her and am immensely grateful for whatever small part I'm allowed to play in her life."

Doctor von Sturm gave me an imposing, disdainful look.

"I don't believe you really think that," she said. "If you are happy, why do you behave with such hostility toward your Mistress? Why do you wet the floor? Why do you chew her slippers?"

I began to answer, but Doctor von Sturm held up her hand. She turned to my Mistress. "I'd say he has a bad case of Venus envy, Burke. As a victim of the inferiority of his sex, he begrudges women for the power they have. He overcompensates with an inflated sense of entitlement."

"Can you shrink him?" asked my Mistress.

"That is up to him," said von Sturm.

The next day I lay on Doctor von Sturm's couch and I told her how much I wanted to please my Mistress and how she was the sole subject of my thoughts when I touched myself.

"You're feel lucky that a woman like Mrs Ketchener would even wipe her feet on you, don't you?"

"Yes," I said. "I guess so."

"But if you really wanted to please her, you wouldn't have failed," she said. "You are here because you've failed. That's all you've been your whole life, a failure. Isn't that right?"

I winced at the question. Her treatment seemed more like brainwashing than medical therapy. I nodded my head.

"You don't seem convinced of it."

"I don't know. One day my Mistress indulges me as her favorite, the next I'm in the doghouse. And yes, sometimes I do think I'm a man and I want her to recognize me as such. Is that wrong?"

"Is it? How do you see yourself? As a man or a mouse?"

"As the most miserable and most happy man on earth," I said.

"Certainly that is not a trivial existence. Why do you say you feel insignificant, that you're good for nothing, an insignificant mouse?"

"I feel immense frustration and immense excitement at the same time. Perhaps I degrade myself by submitting to my Mistress's will, yet a small, but key part of me elevates. My Mistress, not I, is the master of my body. Her own is so magnificent. Any attention she pays me is more than I deserve."

Thus, the hour continued. Educated about the human psyche, Doctor von Sturm had a special talent for brow-beating. By manipulating my need for approval, she put words in my mouth and made me feel thoroughly, ashamed of myself. She seemed to enjoy her work. Toward the end of the session, I noticed that she dropped her left hand and was demurely rubbing herself.

"Good," Doctor von Sturm said at last, looking at her watch. "Time's up. I think we made some progress today, don't you? Of course, you're going to feel worse before you get better. But, before you know it, we'll have you put back together, better than new. I'll see you tomorrow."

I went to Doctor von Sturm daily. I entered therapy as a mouse; after three years of shrinking, I was reduced to half-a-mouse.

As Burke Ketchener's slave, I was merely a tool. As her pet, I represented her.

My Mistress was not content to mold my mind to suit her caprice. She wanted my body to conform to her idea of what a boyish figure should be. With her controlling every morsel of food that went into my mouth, I stayed lean. But, as a coddled creature, I got little exercise.

"This easy life has made you soft," my Mistress said, as she poked me in the belly.

She brought me to the Madison Health Club, a posh fitness center whose clientele was Upper East Side ladies. We had an appointment with a personal trainer recommended by Mrs Harrod.

Grendel Wechsler was blonde, five foot eight and made of iron.

"I want him tight," said my Mistress, "And push him. He's lazy."

"Rest assured, Lady Ketchener," said Grendel. "After a few months you won't even recognize him."

Grendel took her job very seriously. In the first session she put me through a gruelling routine. She carried a dozen keys on a long chain. When I thought I could not do another repetition, she chided me for not making a proper effort. She called me a sissy and hit me with her keys on the buttocks, back and shoulders to get me to exert myself. As I did leg presses, she felt freely in my shorts. She said she was checking to see if I was performing the workout properly.

The Madison Club prided itself on being the epitome of Big Apple polish. There were individual dressing rooms with private Jacuzzis and showers. After the session, Grendel, who worked out vigorously between clients, took me to her dressing room and had me lick her sweaty underarms and crotch before she showered.

I came home pumped up, hard. My Mistress was pleased with the results Grendel was getting. I did not dare talk of my trainer's methods.

Grendel lived up to her promise. After ninety days my body was transformed. I was trimmer and more sculpted than I ever was in my youth.

Of course it was not in my Mistress's nature to be satisfied for long. She abhorred any imperfect reflection on her. Mrs Harrod had been travelling and brought back a new boy, a very pretty Malaysian who couldn't have been more than nineteen. My Mistress became envious and began to express discontent about my face. I was, after all, now nearing forty.

Although my Mistress's beauty would always remain intact in my eyes — indeed the lines forming around her eyes and her mouth showed a decadence that increased her sex appeal — under her double standard, my own subtle signs of aging were unacceptable to her.

For our seventeenth anniversary, she took me to a New York plastic surgeon for a consultation.

"I want him nipped, tucked and tightened," she said. "And while you're at it you might shorten his nose, widen his lips and strengthen his jaw."

She picked out some features from a catalog of photographs, as if she were choosing a new way to style my hair at Monsieur Bari's.

I was terrified of the knife and, more to the point, I was thoroughly attached to myself looking as I did. But when the surgeon presented me with the release form, my Mistress stood over me in her high boots and petted my head. Mouse that I was, I was too weak to refuse. I signed it without a word of protest. I hoped a new nose would at least mean I would no longer have to wear my nose ring.

The surgeon said that the week before Christmas was always slow. He had an opening.

"Perfect!" said my Mistress.

Not wanting to trouble herself with the mess and inconvenience of my recovery from the procedure, she made plans to spend the holidays in Paris at the home of one of her suitors, a man named Alex Rolphe. A hired nurse and Julia would look after me.

I underwent the surgery on the winter solstice and spent Christmas and New Year's in the apartment watching television and worrying. How did I look? I was too terrified to look in a mirror. I prayed to the Goddess my Mistress would be pleased by my new appearance. If she was not, I knew she would not hesitate to send me back to have me fixed to her liking.

She was to arrive on the sixth of January, but she called and said she would not be back until the ninth. She was having her way, making the suspense unbearable.

When she finally arrived, I fell to my hands and knees in front of her and greeted her, wagging my tail and hiding my face in the furry hem of her coat.

She grabbed my hair and pulled my head this way and that to see the job from all angles. She winced with surprise, then she smiled.

"That's more like it," she said.

The mark she left on my shoulder was the outward sign of the inner power she had over me. How much more overwhelming was this new face she had given me!

I finally had the courage to look at myself. The pretty thing I saw looking back at me was a stranger in his late twenties.

Mind and spirit, face and figure, I was my Mistress's creation.

She spent the remainder of that January in New York, going to lunches in the day and attending charity benefits and cultural events in the evenings.

In February she went to East Africa with her old flame Kelman Straub and several other movie stars. They were attempting to alert the world to the plight of children orphaned by the vicious struggle between warring tribes. In her absence, I took the opportunity to continue my diary.

In today's paper there was a picture of her holding a malnourished, fleabitten infant. Does she mean to get attention for the infant or for herself? The image cannot supplant the meaty reality of the woman I know and adore: a tyrannical, carefree monarch who derives pleasure from the devaluation and waste of the people closest to her. I crave her vanquishing embrace.

In the beginning of March, my Mistress returned. On the airplane she had made the acquaintance of a socially prominent playboy named Clement Harmon. He began to pursue her, calling her on the telephone daily. At first she put him off. I heard her tell Mrs Eblis that she thought Harmon was charming, but found him physically unappealing.

"I had that problem with Prince Leopold," said Mrs Eblis. "Before I would see him I would have my boy fluff me."

"*Fluff* you?"

"You know, have a little tease game and then use the excitement of it to seduce Harmon."

Later, Harmon called. My Mistress invited him over for a drink.

She had me lie by her while she prepared for him. She stood naked except for a pair of spike heels, sipping brandy, looking at herself in the vanity mirror. She squeezed her breasts, smelled under her arms and tickled her puss. She had me show my reverence to her ass. When her cheeks begin to flutter and her pleasure was about to erupt, she pushed me away.

Fully aroused, she looked sensational. She doused herself in perfume, and chose a sexy dress with a tight bodice and a long, flowing skirt. The doorbell rang.

She shooed me into the closet and warned me to be still. Then went to let Harmon in.

I heard them talking in the parlor, having a drink. I could not hear what she was saying but I could hear her laughter. The silence of their kiss crashed louder than a bang of thunder.

I was the fluff in their affair. Before she saw Harmon, she always took me in hand and teased herself with me. She would not allow me release. The thought of my discomfort added to her excitement.

I looked forward to summer. I hoped she would see less of Harmon when we were at Lavender Hill. The evening before our departure, my Mistress engaged me in an usually long round of foreplay. We were both consummately aroused when she locked me in her bedroom closet.

Cruel beyond measure, she invited Harmon to her bed. I lay behind two inches of oak listening to them. I could hear his heavy breathing and my Mistress's delicate sighs. The years of therapy notwithstanding, my emotions got the better of me. Rejected, unrequited, I began beating the walls. The commotion interrupted their lovemaking.

Harmon was astonished to learn that she had another man in the closet. He left in a huff. My Mistress slapped me and said, "Bad!"

She locked me in for the night. The next morning, before we were supposed to leave for Lavender Hill, a black car came for me. It was Countess Vladimira's. I was being sent back for a refresher course.

"An obedient little doggie does not limit his Mistress's freedom," Madame Ursulak said when she saw me.

She pulled me over her lap by my nipple rings and gave me an old-fashioned spanking me with her hand. Then she chained me to a tree by the kitchen door with two other boys who had also acted out of turn. I spent the night on the cold ground, unfed. In the morning, Madame Ursulak took us one by one on a leash to relieve ourselves in the woods. In the evening I was brought to the Countess's table. It had been several years since I had seen her. The Countess did not look any older. She brandished a hickory walking stick and lectured me about showing jealousy.

"The next time you are sent back to me for acting up," she said, "it'll be my pleasure to break every jealous bone in your body."

In the meanwhile I was beaten by Madame Ursulak. She had a collection of nasty whips and paddles that made a more lasting impression that Doctor von Sturm's verbal attempt to lick my mind into shape.

The most painful sting came from seeing Ivana going about her chores with a four-year-old boy tied to her apron strings. "This is Alexi Valanescu," Ivana said.

She told me that the Countess had legally adopted the baby after she had given birth. I thought Alexi bore a resemblance to me. Ivana agreed. But she could not be sure. "I am the Countess's breeder. She desperately wanted a daughter, an heir. She wanted me pregnant and made certain it happened. During that period when I was with you, I was thrown into the cages of several of the Countess's trainees."

Ivana told me that after Alexi was born, the Countess knelt before the painting of the Horned God with the infant in her arms and said, "Great Lord, I bring you a new servant."

It was a demonic blessing that I wasn't positive Alexi was my son. Whoever his father was, he was not a free man. One slave is the same as the next. At least with the Countess's name, the boy would be provided for.

"Two years ago the Countess forced me to try again," said Ivana. "This time I managed to produce a daughter."

Unlike Alexi, who was consigned to be his birth mother's little helper, Vladimira II was whisked away to a luxurious nursery upstairs and attended by a trio of nannies, all previously employed by European royalty.

The weather was cool. The week ended with two days of intermittent drizzle. I was chained to a post by the garbage shed, left to shiver in the muck and the mire.

At last, Madame Ursulak brought me in and let me wash. Before the car took me back to my Mistress, the Countess pierced my new nose and outfitted it with a gold ring.

"Don't let me see you here again," she warned and gave a tug to the ring.

I was thrilled to return to Lavender Hill. My Mistress was lounging in bed. I knelt before her and, still feeling the punishment Madame Ursulak inflicted on me, I promised her I had learned my lesson. It was not a week I wanted to repeat. She smiled and followed with an unkinder cut.

"While you were away," she said, "I made up with Mister Harmon. He'll be here in a half-hour. Now come here and fluff me."

She gave a little tug on my new nose ring and lay back. I eagerly went for her. When we heard Harmon's car drive up, she ordered me to go to my quarters and be silent. As I listened to her finishing with Harmon what she started with me, I hardly noticed my resentment.

Harmon was her summer thrill. She broke up with him in September. She seemed sad. I heard her talking on the telephone to Mrs Harrod about how a good man was impossible to find. Through the fall, she sat by the fire, drinking and looking out the window as the leaves changed and fell. She had me stay for hours curled up at her feet. I hoped I was some consolation to her.

In December, when the weather got cooler and the days got short and dark, she decided she needed a change of scenery. She made several calls to real estate agents and rented a home on Sabal Island, Florida, an exclusive spit of land in the intracoastal waterway off Miami Beach.

For the air flight, my Mistress allowed me to remove my nose ring and collar.

The Florida sun was warm and welcoming. The house was stucco and tile, villa-style, airy, comfortably furnished and surrounded by tall palms, hibiscus, jasmine and bougainvillea. Yolanda and Edouardo lived in an apartment over the garage. They did all the chores. Even before unpacking, my Mistress decided to have a drink by the pool. So there would be no doubt in the old couple's minds about the nature of my relationship to the Lady of the House, my Mistress put the ring back in my nose, buckled the leather collar around my neck and had me lie in my shorts at her feet. I was paralyzed with embarrassment. Yolanda tsked her tongue and blessed herself. Shame on me. But Edouardo gave me a wink that said he thought I was a lucky dog.

Soon after we arrived in Florida, my Mistress was invited to tea at Lady Quantrill's in Palm Beach. She decided to bring me along.

I had often heard my Mistress speak of Lady Quantrill, a member of the British peerage whom my Mistress had met when she was married to Barton Ketchener. Like her

Aunt Brittany and Countess Vladimira, Lady Quantrill was an older woman whom my Mistress regarded as a mentor.

My Mistress dressed in a sleeveless black linen dress, leather pumps and a wide-brimmed straw hat. I had never seen her look more handsome. She dressed me in white shorts made of slippery silk and a matching shirt. Before we left, she ordered me to my knees. I knelt at attention while she put my collar on. She lifted her dress and pulled me by the nose ring, pressing the sweet and sour mystery in her panties against my nostrils. I wriggled with excitement. She sighed with pleasure, fully enjoying my adoration.

"Up, boy!" she said. "I just wanted to give you something to think about."

I took a deep breath and followed.

For the ride up to Palm Beach, my Mistress had Edouardo take the coastal highway. I sat in the back seat with her, looking at the passing hotels, towering condominiums and private mansions with green lawns and lush tropical vegetation. Whenever she saw me start to flag she would touch me and bring me to a full swell again. I saw Edouardo looking at us in the rear-view mirror. I always felt like a fool in my nose ring and collar.

Lady Quantrill lived in a palace of Italian marble and Spanish tile. We pulled into a drive of English cobblestone and parked near a fountain. Water trickled from the mouth of a marble lion. A dark, muscular, barefoot Latino in black velvet tap pants and a ruffled white shirt appeared immediately. Evidently he had been awaiting our arrival. The boy escorted us inside to a sitting room which opened onto a weathered marble court with another fountain surrounded by large ferns, tropical ginger and orchids.

A mature woman appeared from the far door. Lady Quantrill's extreme femininity, elegant style and air of experience gave her an ageless beauty. Her skin and hair were golden white, smooth, and soft as her platinum jewelry. She wore brown heels, a brown skirt and a white blouse with billowy sleeves and a plunging neckline that revealed the tops of her still voluptuous breasts. She carried a small dog in the crook of her left arm. My Mistress kissed Lady Quantrill warmly and the two exchanged greetings.

"His name is Vajra!" said Lady Quantrill, introducing her pet. The Lhasa gave a shrill bark when he heard his name. My Mistress admired the little beast and stroked his head.

My Mistress and Lady Quantrill each inquired about the other's health and well-being. As usual, the pleasantries were soon replaced by nasty gossip about other women and news and analyses of their latest sexual conquests.

"I stay with my slaves now, exclusively," said Lady Quantrill, as she walked over to the Latino standing at attention and pinched the bulge in his hotpants. She pulled a cord and a second boy appeared, a short, slim Asian dressed in a transparent cotton shirt and pants. He also bowed to his Mistress, then to mine, and took his place at attention behind Lady Quantrill, beside his fellow.

I shifted nervously from one foot to another, burning with jealousy as my Mistress described a recent dalliance, unknown to me, with a man named Raffaello. I was further tormented by the length of time the ladies chatted, leaving me standing and completely ignored. I did my best to appear patient and hoped my disquiet went unnoticed. I wanted to reflect well on my Mistress and make a good impression. My love for her was showing, pressing against my shorts. My juices were seeping, making a wet spot in the light silk. I was unsure whether my Mistress would be proud or ashamed of this conspicuous display.

At this point, the ladies began to whisper. I wondered if they were talking about me.

Lady Quantrill turned and looked at me for the first time. She noted the protrusion and the stain. She gave me a bold, commanding smile that heightened my embarrassment.

I bowed to her. "My Mistress has spoken of you often, Lady," I said. "I am honored to meet you."

Lady Quantrill laughed softly. "Indeed you are."

She motioned to a pair of roomy wing chairs in a cozy nook and asked my Mistress to sit with her. She looked at me and gestured to a small sofa in the opposite corner of the room. That was where I was to sit.

My Mistress and Lady Quantrill did not look at me or include me in their conversation. They spoke quietly, and because I was at a distance, I could only hear part of what they were saying. It was just as well, I thought.

The sofa was not the sort one could sink into. The seat and the back were cushioned with stiff padding and upholstered with smooth silk. My shorts and shirt, loose, made of similar material, had me sliding uncomfortably forward and to the side. My shorts rode up. My erection hampered my efforts to pull them down.

The Asian boy left and came back with tea, cakes and a carafe of cognac. Lady Quantrill poured and asked my Mistress if she would like some of the liquor.

"Yes, thank you," said my Mistress.

"And what about your pet? Do you allow him alcohol?"

"Not when we're visiting. It makes him too talkative."

"Perhaps he would like some milk then," said Lady Quantrill. She placed a china saucer down at her heel and poured from the creamer into it. "My dear," she said to my Mistress, "Please, have your pet come here and lap this milk."

My Mistress turned to me and said, "Boy, do you hear Lady Quantrill?"

I realized I was being tested. A wayward notion outbid my desire to make a good impression. Seated and dressed uncomfortably as I was, tossing on a sea of jealousy, embarrassment and arousal, I became resentful. For some perverse reason — or was it a shred of self-esteem? —I decided to show Lady Quantrill that I still had some independent spirit left. I stood up to my Mistress by staying on the divan.

"Boy, did you hear me?" my Mistress said, this time with an insistent edge in her voice. "You will get down and lap this milk."

I could not.

Lady Quantrill raised her eyebrows. "I'll take care of you when we get home," my Mistress said stiffly. Then she turned from me and went back to sipping tea and cognac.

My gambit of playing the fussy pet backfired. I was in the doghouse. The women talked for a couple of hours and said nothing further to me.

We left Palm Beach just as the sun was setting. For the return ride to Miami, my Mistress had Edouardo take the expressway. I sat in the back seat with her. I longed for her to touch me or to speak, even to frown or reprimand me, but there was only an icy silence. My Mistress was deciding my fate. I could feel her annoyance with me mount. I did not know what to expect. Would I be sent away? The thought terrified me. I prayed to the Goddess she would forgive me.

When we arrived home, my Mistress ordered me to her bedroom. She had me undress and get on my hands and knees. She attached the chains to my body rings and, using small padlocks, secured me to the brass rail at the foot of her bed. I was unable to move more than an inch up, down or to the sides.

I understood I was to be punished and wanted to show her I could take it like a man. Given how I was tied, I had not much choice.

"Bad boy!" she shouted as she hit me with the leash.

"You will ne-ver, ne-ver, ne-ver, ne-ver, ne-ver, dis-o-bey me a-gain. Do you un-der-stand?"

She struck me to accent every syllable. By the second "never" I was in tears, my buttocks and thighs in flames.

"Yes, yes, I swear," I sobbed. "Please, no more."

"You will re-mem-ber this, won't you?" She gave me another round for good measure.

I spent the night on my hands and knees, chained to my Mistress's bed frame. When I began to doze, I would slump down, the rings would pull on my skin and I would wake up.

The following morning Edouardo brought coffee and left it in the sitting room outside my Mistress's bedroom. Before going to it, she unchained me and allowed me to use the water closet. When I returned, I crept up to her. I praised her for her leniency and patience and asked if she would let me sit by her feet as she sipped her coffee.

"No!" she snapped and kicked me away.

I was still in the doghouse.

The telephone rang. It was Lady Quantrill. She had plans to come to Miami Beach for shopping. Did my Mistress want to join her?

Two hours later Lady Quantrill arrived, driven by her Asian boy. My Mistress led me down on a leash. Edouardo was serving coffee to Lady Quantrill on the patio. My Mistress took the saucer from under her cup, set it down by Lady Quantrill's heel and poured from the creamer into it. I instantly went to my knees and lapped up every drop.

One evening in late February, my Mistress attended a benefit to help send food and medical aid to Haiti. I dozed on the fleecy goatskin throw-rug by her bed. Just after midnight I heard her arrive. I loved to sit on the floor and watch her as she undressed and went through her bedtime beauty rituals. Sometimes, if she was feeling kind, she would toss me her panties. My mouth began to water. I perked up, puffed up, and waited to greet her.

But I was taken aback when she entered the room. She had a boy with her. He was Haitian, very dark and very pretty, with high cheekbones and a downcast look in his eye.

"I thought you must get lonely, Mouse," she said. "This is Alfonse. He was working as a server and I took a fancy to him. He'll be a nice playmate for you, won't he?"

I tried not to let my vexation show, but it was more than I could do to suppress it. I snarled.

"Mouse! You're going to have to learn to mind your manners."

My first impression was that Alfonse was a simple, gentle creature, overwhelmed to be in the bedroom of an elegant American lady. But he was not shy. He knew what to do. He seemed quite willing to play her game. He took off his clothes, got down on the floor next to me and began wagging his tail and cooing in patois.

"Good Alfonse! Smart Alfonse!" she said.

"The Mistress likes to see her pets getting along with one another," she said with a playful smile. "Mouse, I want to see you give Alfonse a kiss on the mouth."

I pulled my head back, repelled. Her suggestion was heinous, diabolical. I saw Alfonse's face fall. But after a moment's hesitation, he moved closer to me, closed his eyes and puckered up. He had a dogged eagerness to please her, no matter how much her game degraded him. I craved her approval, too. I hated the idea of her thinking he was a better man than I. In order to compete with him, I had to be accommodating.

I closed my eyes and brushed my lips to Alfonse's.

"Now touch one another."

I felt Alfonse's delicate, bold fingers on me. I touched him timidly. My Mistress gave a little sigh. I glanced up at her. She was all eyes and touching herself.

"Here, Alfonse." She patted the edge of her bed and had him jump up.

I begged her to consider my feelings. She laughed. When I became more insistent, she slapped me on the head and told me to hold my tongue. To enforce her order she removed her panties and stuffed them into my mouth. Then she had Alfonse service her in front of me. Watching them, I felt an unbearable agony.

She had Alfonse sleep in her bed and me lie, gagged, on the floor beside the bed.

I spent the night listening to the stirring above me. In the eighteen years we had been together, she never once allowed me to sleep with her.

In the morning she relieved me of the gag, which made my mouth very dry. Even though I was furious I tried not to sulk. I choked out my thanks and praised her for her mercy. She left me alone in the room with Alfonse while she bathed and dressed.

Alfonse, unpretentious as he was, spoke English much better than he let my Mistress understand. "Excuse me if I have caused you distress, my friend," he said to me with a bright smile. "But I must make my living however I can. I find catering to the personal needs of wealthy ladies easier and more lucrative than waiting on tables."

"Did my Mistress pay you?"

"Five hundred dollars. It's not much, considering. I am not naive about the decadence of the rich. How much food I see them waste at these benefits to help starving children!"

Yolanda brought my Mistress her breakfast in the sitting room. My Mistress summoned Alfonse and me. She began

174

to tease us, holding up strips of bacon, expecting us to beg. Alfonse put on an entertaining show, but, as much as I wanted to, I was too hurt to indulge my Mistress's caprice. Sensing I was losing the rivalry, I was hit with a wave of jealousy and lost control. "Monster!" I screamed and turned the table over, throwing the food and the setting to the floor. Certainly a servant who destroys his Mistress's property might be dismissed without further discussion. And a vicious house pet? Sent to the pound, perhaps destroyed.

The tantrum subsided as quickly as it arose. I most humbly begged her forgiveness. But she said nothing. She sneered, rose, taking Alfonse to attend her at her dressing table. I remained on the floor of the sitting room paralyzed with fear of what my punishment would be.

My Mistress walked over me on her way out. "Mouse," she fumed, "I'm going out shopping. When I get back I don't expect to find you here. Come, Alfonse, I'll need you to carry my packages."

I felt myself fallen under a death sentence. My Mistress was as important to me as air, as water, as food. Without her, I would die.

When she left, I went to her bed like a zombie. There was a wet stain on the sheets where she lay. I fell on it. Her piss and honey scent was still fresh. It drove me wild. I began to rub myself.

Suddenly I heard a sound. I turned around and there was my Mistress standing over me, alone. She had forgotten her sunglasses. I fell to the floor and crept to her on all fours.

"Beat me!" I shed tears on her shoes. "Burn me! Cut me! But, whatever you do, don't turn me away."

She lifted her foot and brought the heel down firmly on my neck. I felt pangs of delight as she ground me down. She grew excited too. Without further ado, she drew me back to the bed, raised her skirt and took me. When it was over she kissed me softly and said, "I don't really want you to leave."

She led me by the collar to the closet. Before she tossed me in, she kissed me again and said, "The only reason I brought Alfonse home was to get a rise out of you. I love *you*, you fool, and only you. And I'll always love you."

And with that she pushed me into the darkness and bolted the door behind me.

Although my body was interred, my soul was in heaven. She said she loved me. She said she loved me. She said she'd always love me. I repeated this all day until I heard her return. When she unlocked the closet, I crawled to her. She had sent Alfonse away. She still had me.

My Mistress informed me that I was to accompany her to La Columbe, a fashionable restaurant, *the* place to be seen in Miami. I could not believe my ears. To be her escort was a privilege I had so long and so fondly dreamed of. She removed my body rings and my collar.

"A well-trained pet behaves properly without constraints," she said and kissed me. "Anyway, you're more than a pet, you're a love."

I glowed.

We made our entrance at La Columbe just after eight. As Laurent the maitre d' escorted us to our table, a woman with a British accent, sitting with a large party, called out, "Burke, darling!" My Mistress left me with Laurent and went over to chat. She seemed to be acquainted with everybody at the table. I was hurt that she didn't introduce me. However, I understood. She could not see herself except as reflected by others. She wanted to be attached to those who radiated power, wealth and celebrity, not to a man she met in a grocery store. The men looked sideways at me. The women adjusted their eyeglasses. In my imagination, I still wore the rings and the collar. I felt that my position as her underling was obvious to all. I stood there making self-conscious small talk with Laurent until she finished her conversation.

We sat at a banquette table, she on the inside. She ordered for the both of us. Throughout the meal, she corrected my table manners in a stern whisper.

"Sit up straight!"

"No! Not that fork!"

"Don't eat so fast!"

"There had better not be a spot on that suit!"

Then suddenly, for no apparent reason, when dessert and after-dinner drinks arrived, she became tender again. She patted the banquette seat and asked me to move next to her. She put her hand on the nape of my neck and whispered softly in my ear, "After all these years, Mouse, I finally can admit it. I don't care who's watching or what they think. I love you. I can't wait to get you home." She turned my head to her and kissed me.

I was ready to leave the restaurant whenever she was. But my Mistress invited her chatty friend to our table for a drink. Tanya Spar was visiting from London. I intended to maintain a respectful silence as the women gossiped but the cognac got my tongue. I made a few humorous observations. My contributions amused Tanya and when my Mistress did not rebuff me I began inserting remarks more frequently. Soon we were a jolly trio. My Mistress appeared to enjoy having me by her side. I felt her approval when I spoke. She petted my thigh under the table.

Back at the house, my Mistress threw me on the bed and, without saying a word, made love to me with wild abandon. Afterwards, I kissed her and said, "How thrilling! I feel we are at last truly intimate, that we can share a wonderful love." I hoped she would respond in kind. But again her mood shifted. She became incensed. When I begged her forgiveness for my remarks, she gave a jab to my nose that made me see stars. She told me to stay in the guest room.

In the morning I was walking on eggshells. She stayed in her room until afternoon. When she came out, I steeled myself for further rebuke, but she smiled sweetly at me.

"I don't know what came over me," she said. "I do love you. But I have my moods, you know. I hope you can forgive me for hitting you like that."

"It's me who should beg your forgiveness, Madam. I was such a fool to ruin a beautiful moment by talking about it."

She took me to her bedroom. Again she gave every indication of enjoying the lovemaking as much as I. I did not presume to comment. We had a quiet dinner. Then she took me to bed again. For the first time ever, we spent the night together.

For the remainder of our days in Miami she was mellow, seductive and warm to me. The tenderness continued when we went back north. We celebrated Easter together in Manhattan and spent the summer at Lavender Hill. She surprised me with an electronic notebook. Feeling her love for me, I had less need for the outlet that putting my feelings on paper provided. But she insisted.

"I don't want you only writing about the bad times," she said.

By day, we strolled the trails through the hills or along the winding Housatonic, going arm-in-arm or holding hands. At night, we would lie in bed, listening to the crickets. I would tell her of my great love for her and she would pet me until I came in her hands or in her puss.

In September, the nights were chilly. I would light a fire and she would cuddle close, whispering her darkest domination fantasies in my ear. I would assent to being her servile captive. Joined by our reciprocal imaginations, we locked in playful, exhilarating embraces.

On October mornings, after breakfasts of English tea, French bread and Swiss chocolate, we would walk through the woods, enjoying the colors, the crispy clarity, the coolness, and the crunch of the hoarfrost on the fallen leaves and pine needles under our boots. Our favorite spot to feel the world at peace was the jutting edge of Cobblers' Ridge where we had a grand view of the Litchfield Hills and the Berkshires beyond them. We would sit out of the wind and watch the clouds and the vibrant autumn foliage, marvelling at the changes of heaven and earth, laughing, kissing and fumbling in one another's woolen pants.

"The greatest wonder of all," she purred, "is that you are the other half of my soul. You were there all along, but I was blind."

We shared. We cared. We bared our hearts. These were the happiest moments of my existence. At long last, I was the man in my Mistress's life.

My dream had come true. My Mistress was my best friend and my lover. But was this serenity merely a prelude to my worst nightmare? No man lasted long in her affection. And however intimate our relationship had become, it sat on a lop-sided foundation. While I had lost myself in fantasies of unlimited powerlessness, she remained preoccupied by a grandiose sense of self-importance. In our complementary minds' eyes, she was entitled to everything and I was entitled to nothing. She elevated men to plunge them down. Seduced, I was ripe for abandonment.

Toward the end of the month, I sensed a growing distance in her. I told her my fears and asked her about her intentions. Was she exhausting a new possibility of violating me? Was there someone else? Was she setting me up for the biggest fall yet?

She did not reply directly to my questions but reprimanded me for not believing in her.

My happiness unravelled on Halloween night. She walked by me on her way out, dressed in a skin-tight, red satin devil's costume, complete with horns, barbed tail and small pitch fork. She did not even look in my direction. I had the whole thrust of biological and psychological evolution telling me to be possessive of my mate. I stopped her and asked her where she was going.

She pulled away from me, menaced me with the fork and left the house.

I waited for her in a state of high anxiety. She did not return until the following afternoon. By that time I was a nervous wreck.

I went to her and I apologized for forgetting my place.

"I'm not in the mood for you now," she said, pushing me aside. "I'm tired."

She went upstairs to her rooms.

For two days she remained aloof. I had worked so hard to secure my Mistress's affections that I became hysterical over the loss of them. On the evening of the third day, I was in my quarters when suddenly the door opened. She was standing over me, twirling a pair of her panties around her finger.

She pushed me face down on the bed and put the panties over my face. She had had them on earlier and they reeked of her femininity. Then she got on my back and took my testicles in her soft, strong hands. I bucked gently as I had been trained. I relaxed in the rhythm of her movement. She jockeyed herself on me until she had her pleasure.

Then she whispered, "How dare you question me, boy? You must *never* challenge your Mistress."

I apologized.

She grunted with irritation and squeezed my most delicate parts. I curled up, out of breath, and rolled off the bed onto the floor from the pain. My Mistress rose.

"I will do as I like," she said harshly. "I do not need your advice. *I* do not answer to *you*."

She left me on the floor, winded, clutching myself in agony. My nose was still in her panties.

It was a cruel and unusual punishment, physically painful and psychologically devastating. The following morning I was still in great discomfort. I went to my Mistress, knelt and begged her forgiveness.

"Madam, you must excuse me. I became confused. Since you were being so friendly the past months, I forgot my place. I no longer know who I am."

"You are what I say you are."

I was what she said I was: her slave, her playmate, her lover, her boy, her man, her mouse, her pussy, her puppy, her fall guy, her bugaboo, her toy, her beast, her whore, her thing, her chronicler, the keeper of her cock and balls.

Both Christianity and pagan religion see the spirit of God taking abode in a fleshy container. But while the Christian believes that God sacrificed himself once for all, the Goddess worshipper believes that the Divine Victim comes in different forms, in different times and places. He must sacrifice himself over and over again.

I did not truly understand sacrifice when I committed myself to the Muse. Over the years I learned that for my resignation to be acceptable to her, it had to be continual. She needed to have me renew my vows, to will my submission to her again and again. This meant she had to break me again and again. Seduced and abandoned, I was ripe for re-seduction. Slain and reborn, I was ready to be sacrificed anew.

That Christmas, my Mistress bought a small estate named Malden in the nearby town of Lawton's Bridge. While she went to Saint Barth's with a man named Moreau, she left me in the house to oversee the renovations and make sure it was decorated to her taste.

Now when my Mistress wanted privacy, became interested in another man or simply wanted to cause me pain, she had a place to send me. She set me free, but kept me within her domain so she could catch me anew. Each time I was dismissed, the agony became more unbearable. I would sit at Malden brooding over whether I thought she loved me or she loved me not. I would wait, be it for hours, days or months, until the telephone rang. When I heard her voice, all the pain I suffered in her absence was instantly erased.

"Boy?"

"Yes, Madam!"

"Madam didn't mean to hurt you. But she needed time for herself."

"Yes, Madam! Of course. I've missed you enormously."

"You've been playing with yourself, haven't you?"

She knew.

"Bad, bad boy!" she chided. "Madam knows what's best for you. And she loves you. She really does. She's trying to make something out of you. And all you do is fight her. Maybe if you weren't so willful, she might find you more worth her while. But you're really not worthy of her, you know. Most of the time you're perfectly useless. Maybe, this time, she doesn't want you back."

"Madam," I choked, crushed, "please! Give me another chance. I will apply myself. I won't be headstrong. I won't disappoint you. I promise."

"All right, impudent Mouse," she sighed, as if going against her better judgment. "Lucky for you, she's feeling wicked. She expects you here in an hour."

Thus the vicious cycle rolled on. Four more years passed. Under her black magic spell, she made me disappear and reappear. Now I saw her; now I didn't. Each time I returned from Malden to her service, it was with a fresh negation of myself, deeper humiliation and increased devotion.

As my Mistress entered menopause, her face dropped and her body sagged. Her skin, once pink and juicy, became gray and dry. The sparkle in her eyes took on a dull, bloodshot cast. Cosmetic surgery could smooth her wrinkles, but not her cares. Nor could it undo the long-term effects of her bad habits. She could no longer conceal her grand self-doubt in the frivolity of youth. Image, style and puffed-up pretenses could not quell the fear of being beyond repair which gnawed on her.

She gained a few pounds and became obsessively worried about her weight. She overreacted, dieting until she became skeletal. Unable to eat, she tried to fill her empty soul with a glut of appearances, purchasing more clothing and cosmetics than she could ever use. They were little help.

Having only concerned herself with being seen with the right people, she had few life-long close friends. Mrs Eblis had remarried and moved to Ibiza. Mrs Harrod, now in her seventies, was batty. She was alone. She had to face herself.

She would spend hours sitting at her vanity, looking in the mirror, a study in desperation, yanking at her tussled hair with her bony fingers. She would allow me to kneel next to her. While I massaged lotion into the gooseflesh on her calves and feet, she cursed me without reason.

Objectively, my Mistress was no longer a pretty picture. However there was no diminishing the inner power she exerted over me or the physical attraction I felt for her. Like all addictions, over time mine became stronger. I was her votary, body and soul, more ardent than ever.

"I could look at you until the end of time and never get tired," I said, trying to reassure her of my feelings. "You're the most beautiful woman in the world and I'm the luckiest man in the world to be here with you. When I'm near you, even if you're torturing me, I feel the boundless joy of the Divine presence. The love in my spirit can never grow old."

"Fuck you!" she sneered. "You don't mean that, you lazy whore." She accused me of being the cause of her wasted life. She breathed cigarette smoke in my face, and poured herself another drink.

The older the witch, the meaner. A difficult woman to begin with, my Mistress became impossible, a dragon lady hell-bent on destroying herself and everything around her.

"If only you loved yourself as I love you," I said.

"Love?" she gulped her drink. "What's that? Come and fuck me!"

She needed me to lean on while she walked to bed.

In intimacy, where she once shined supremely beautiful, now she looked down on me with a haggish countenance. But I was not repulsed. In her consuming embrace, spurred by my inexhaustible devotion and my urgent need to please, I was as stiff and juicy as a teenage boy.

She bubbled over with excitement and fell dead-asleep on top of me, snoring and drooling. I lay under her, sleepless, quiet as a mouse. She woke with hot flashes and cold sweats, and looked at me as if I were the specter of death.

I skulked off, berating myself for not making her happier. But a few hours later, when she found a new wrinkle, she called me in a vain attempt to smooth it.

Orgasm helped her escape her preoccupation with decline. She became sexually hyperactive. Several times a day, she threw me on her bed and made love to me with an impatient fierceness. The hungry cat pounced with wild abandon, exhausting the mouse. When I couldn't satisfy her, she cursed me.

"What the fuck is wrong with you?" she growled. "Don't you love me?"

"Yes, Madam, I do. I adore you."

"Why don't you show it?" She gave her overworked mouse a swat.

"I'm only capable of so much."

"You're self-involved, that's the problem."

She hated me for loving her, yet, paradoxically, demanded my complete, irrational, unremitting devotion. She slapped me. On conditioned reflex, the proof of my passion began to rise.

She glared at me and looked away.

"What's wrong now?" I asked. "Isn't this what you wanted?"

"You're a whore. Name your price first."

"I don't want money. I want you to make love to me."

"Who do you think you are? I keep you for your services. Now what's your price?"

"Is money all you can think about? After all this time, don't *I* matter to you at all?"

"Not really. And now your insolence puts me out of the mood."

Could she know what was in my heart, how open I was to her, how vulnerable, how much I loved her? The boundaries my Mistress set for me and the physical, mental and emotional tortures she inflicted were essential ingredients of her gratification. She regarded any sympathetic feelings, any tenderness toward me, as faults, aberrations to be rooted out of the controlled caprice that was her life. Her heart, so long held in check, was withering. She clung to her desire for me but she resented it too. As a defense, she felt rage. She was angry because she could not stand alone. Yet she was not alone. She had every means at her disposal to annihilate her boredom, yet time and again she chose me as her idle pleasure. I stayed when so many others came and went. I had been a constant in her life. Indeed we were a couple, and a very well-matched one at that.

Every year the warm weather brought a greater influx of tourists to Norbury. Boorish crowds and traffic jangled my Mistress's already unsteady nerves.

"Pack your things, Mouse. We're going to New York."

We passed our twenty-third summer together in her town house. Her Majesty confined me to a back bedroom. Some nights, she would go out and not return. Other nights, she would have a visitor. Nevertheless she still summoned me two or three times a day for the servicing her high-strung condition required.

She was more unhappy than ever, and I had to suffer. She took every discomfort and annoyance out on me. She changed her mind incessantly. Everything I did was wrong. One of her favorite games was to dangle some substantial intimacy, such as suggesting we go on an exotic vacation together, and then take it away at the last minute. She would fuck me and then become a vicious harpy who tore me apart. Every day she found a way to disappoint me. If there was no spontaneous opportunity to frustrate my devotion, she would go out of her way to manufacture one. She didn't need to earn my love, but why did she have to do everything possible to thwart it? If only she would allow me to do what I was born to do!

The wounds she inflicted were deep but they did not kill the love I felt for her. If anything, they added to her allure.

Late August, the city was quiet. Her mood brightened. She became pleasant. The other man seemed out of her life. Every night we would dine at the Mayfair. One evening, coming home, as we strolled along Fifth Avenue, she slid her arm around mine.

"I've been thinking of that summer we spent hiking and making love. I've been a fool treating you as I do."

"No," I said, "it's my fault. I shouldn't have so many expectations."

"Next week will be our twenty-fourth Labor Day together," she said. "Let's go to Paris and celebrate."

I was thrilled to hear it, yet I had my fears, too. I had been disenchanted many times. My suspicion showed.

"Silly boy," she said. "This time I really mean what I say. I'll make the arrangements. We'll leave tomorrow night."

I put my things together. I helped my Mistress with hers. Late in the afternoon, the car arrived. I became enormously excited. The trip seemed as if it would really happen. My Mistress asked me to fetch her bags from her room and went out ahead of me. When I arrived on the street I was stunned to see a man in the backseat of the car.

She was about to get in.

"Who is he?"

"That's none of your business, Mouse."

"You said you were taking *me* with you."

She raised her eyebrows and laughed wickedly.

"Really now? Did I say that? If I did, you were a little fool to believe me. What did you expect? Now kiss me goodbye." She turned a cold cheek to me. "Quickly. I don't want to be late."

I stood speechless.

She withdrew her hand and said sharply, "How fucking rude! It's your discourteous behavior that makes me want to get away from you." She got into the car. The driver closed the door.

"Oh, I almost forgot," she snickered through the open window. "Happy anniversary!" Then she turned and kissed the man and began to chatter animatedly to him as the car pulled away.

In tears, I stormed back into the house. No longer would I indulge my passion for this manipulating, demoralizing and exploitive woman. My things were packed. But when I tried to walk out the door, I felt my Mistress's presence surrounding me, sucking me back, locking me in. Her domain was larger than the New York apartment, Lavender Hill and Malden. As the moon ruled the tides, my Mistress ruled my blood. In the innermost chambers of my cells, I was hers. Immobilized by despair, I stayed. I thought of her all day; I dreamed of her all night.

A week later the Holy Terror returned. She found me lying on my bed sulking. Horrible and enchanting, smelling of French perfume and cognac, she flung herself on top of me and bit my ear. "Is this the way you greet me? Lazy prick! Even though you show such disrespect, I have a reward for you: a week's worth of my stockings, bras and panties to wash. Hop to it!"

I had no will to resist her.

Her dehumanization of me left her faced with an isolation, an emptiness greater than ordinary boredom. She felt alone because the person she was with was no person at all. Where was the pleasure in conquering something that had been so completely conquered? How could she exult in defeating my resolve, if I had no resolve? I thoroughly adored her. But how stimulating to her was adoration by a powerless object? Her control became self-defeating. Just as she overpowered me with her untouchability, she felt overpowered by my vulnerability and in danger of becoming a will-less slave herself. Ironically, for all she suppressed me, she was less of an individual than I.

My writing continued to be the one area where I retained my independence. Internally I enjoyed the freedom my external life lacked. I now had my draft on disc. Looking over my reminiscences, I found myself absorbed as much in fantasies as in facts. I revised and edited the text, turning metaphors to describe our interlocking desires for submission and dominance. Hoping that fulfillment would follow my wish, I ventured to conclude my story. I experimented with endings, happy, sad and in-between. In some versions she was rehabilitated and came to love and respect me. In others she remained a beast. Over the years, my Mistress's alternating moods of grandiosity and melancholy had rubbed off on me. Now they infused my quandary. An insurgent sense of self-worth prompted me to have my hero redeemed by his experiences; the old dog in my emotions craved further debasement. Who would win the battle for my soul? Who did I want to win? The answer eluded me.

My Mistress knew everything that was in my heart. "When are you going to learn," she raged, "You can't explain love. I am who I am, not who you want me to be. Give up!"

I should have been defeated hearing this, but, paradoxically, I was not. I read the anger in her voice as a sign that she was jealous of my unending devotion to my work. She felt threatened by this part of me not under her control, and she had forebodings about the portrait of her which I conjured with my words. She, in the flesh, had to be my only source of pleasure, a perplexing wonder no words could describe.

Momentarily empowered, I saw my hero in a positive light. He was the eternal boy, the worldly philosopher, the mystic lover, the friend to all women, the reckless youth persistent in his folly who becomes the master, the winner who braves the depths of his passion and lives to laugh at himself when he tells about it . . .

Countless times I pledged to accept my fate, no matter how demeaning. What had it gotten me but confusion and heartbreak? My faith in the Muse, weakened through years of being deemed undeserving of recognition and being denied humane treatment, collapsed. I discontinued my supplication. Better late than never, I weaned myself from that cold teat and left her so I might seek encouraging company.

My mind was made up. I would make my exit the following morning before dawn. But in the clear light of day, I realized I was not going anywhere. I returned to my work. I had jumped to a hasty conclusion, using bombast to hide my shame. Now I felt chagrin for erecting such a pawn as a protagonist. Who was I trying to fool? I was nothing but a pampered, whining house pet, bent to serve my Mistress in order to avoid the responsibility for taking care of myself. I was lucky to have her.

In the end, all I had was my addiction to my Mistress. I was not in control. I could not cure myself of this illness. It would have to be the disease that freed me. And I feared health more than death. With my Mistress running the show, unpredictable as she was, anything could happen. She would have the last word.

An emptiness, a kind of post-partum depression, came over me. I felt the need to cling to my Mistress more desperately than ever. She knew my heart. It pleased her to know that I had at last become entirely hers, that she was more necessary to me than the words by which I sought to define her.

Now there was nothing left to take. She had sucked all the juice from me. It was time to spit out the pulp.

Labor Day, the anniversary of my twenty-fifth year in her service, was sweltering hot. The grande dame, a portrait in decadence, was sitting topless by the pool, drinking champagne and eating chocolates. In a congenial mood, she invited me to sit on the lounge next to her.

"Twenty-five years!" she said. "I know I haven't always been easy. What a good boy you've been! You should get a gold watch."

Although I had every reason to be skeptical, I was elated. While she sunbathed, I lay back soaking up the warmth of her kind notice.

She sat up, picked up the telephone and dialed.

"Hello, Henri? This is Burke Ketchener . . . Very well. And you? . . . Happy to hear it . . . You have a waiter there, a pretty boy with long blond hair. He served me last week . . . Roger, is it? . . . Yes. Well, I found him quite appealing. I want him . . . It wouldn't be a problem for you to replace him, would it? . . . Good. I've taken the liberty to send you several boxes of those Cuban coronas you like so much . . . You're quite welcome, Monsieur. Perhaps you could send the boy here tonight with my dinner. Let's see. I'll have a green salad and the lamb . . . Thank you, Henri. Ciao."

"A new boy?" I asked.

The corners of her mouth widened into a wicked smile.

"You just told me how pleased you were with me," I cried. "Anytime you make me feel worthwhile, without fail you have to spoil it. You're evil!"

"When are you going to learn, fool? Life's more fun that way. You love me when I'm being bad, don't you?"

"I do and I don't!"

"Really? Well, I won't have an unpredictable lover. Go! And this time I don't mean to Malden. I want you out of my life entirely, forever."

Although for years I had considered leaving her, this total rejection caught me by surprise. I saw my deepest fear materializing, my future crumbling. My mind crashed. My heart went to pieces. I threw myself on my knees in front of her, begging her to reconsider. She could have Roger or whomever else she wanted. I would not complain.

"You're making me angry now!" she said coldly. "I'm tired of you. I want you out of my sight!"

I knelt there in shock, unable to move.

She took a long, slow swallow of champagne, slid out of her silk shorts and turned over on her stomach. She selected a candy and placed it between her buttocks. With the hot sun and the heat of her body, the chocolate melted and released its cherry cordial filling.

"Eat, Mouse!" she said. "Clean your Mistress! If you please her, she might keep you."

I pressed my tongue to her rear. Mixing with her perspiration and my saliva, the sweet brown-red liquid spread thin and ran deep into the folds of her buttocks and vagina. Several times she came to ecstacy and pushed her candy ass forcefully into my open mouth.

When I licked her clean of every trace of the sticky pap, she turned over and smiled at me. "That's a good boy!"

"For better or for worse, I want to be with you, Madam," I whispered, "Until death do us part. I'm yours."

"And I'm yours too, Mouse." She kissed me.

I breathed a sigh of relief.

"But I don't *want* to be yours," she snapped. "I can no longer abide such presumption from you. Your presence is too great in my life; I feel smothered by you. I've made up my mind. I want you out of here. Entirely, forever. That is my final decision. Goodbye. I wish you the best."

"But you are the best!"

"I'm flattered. But get out!"

"No!"

"Yes!" As changeable as she was, I could now feel her fixed intent. Her heart was hardened against me. "Out!" She put on her robe and left me, kneeling by her chaise.

I worshipped my Mistress. I believed that she was an all-powerful being. To be cast out of her presence was akin to being sentenced to hell. My suffering was so intense that I prayed to both God and Goddess, whoever would listen, to take me from this earth. I would rather be dead than live without her.

But my life went on.

I took a room at the Mount Baden Lodge. I found work as a cook in the restaurant.

After some months, my Mistress sent me a gold watch. It was not inscribed. There was no card or other indication of appreciation with it. It was just a hunk of shiny metal and jeweled clockworks. I was never more to her than this: a lump of matter that moved.

I sold the watch and used the money to relocate. I found a small sublet above a grocery on Fourteenth Street in New York City. I thought of Judith Christian, the literary agent who had once expressed interest in my work. I called her.

"What a nice surprise!" she said when she heard my

voice. "I still have fond memories of our time in Miami." She invited me to her apartment for dinner.

The years had been gentle with Judith. Her spirit had continued to open. When I told her my sad tale, she expressed her sympathy. "You did me a good turn when my heart was breaking," she said. "Now it's time for me to pay you back." She kissed me warmly and invited me to her bed.

We began an affair. Judith was supportive and perceptive, consistently vivacious and good-humored. She understood my pain and did not pressure me. She made me feel safe, whole and satisfied rather than exposed and empty inside. Being in such a nourishing atmosphere helped me piece together my broken heart. Her love gave me the strength to begin to love myself.

My misgivings about showing my memoirs did not prevent me from putting some finishing touches on them. I had briefly told Judith the gist of it. She was fascinated by the idea. She said that, if I wanted, she would be happy to read the text with an eye to representing it. She knew of several publishers who would be eager to see the diary of Burke Ketchener's love slave.

My pagan love story was as ready as it ever would be, but I was reluctant to show it to her. Not only was I ashamed to reveal being such a bad boy at heart, I thought the explicitness of the text might put stress on our relationship. If Judith knew the extent of the sick appetite Burke aroused in me, would she feel sorry for me? Or would she feel hurt, jealous that she did not inspire the same obsession?

On the other hand, what if, as Judith thought, the manuscript had commercial appeal? Wouldn't this public confession of my wayward soul be an open invitation for the worst sort of embarrassment? Would it cause brazen adventuresses to seek me out? No doubt Burke would hear of it and perhaps she would read it. What good could come from that?

I never discussed these concerns with Judith, but she understood. "You should be proud of yourself," she said. "You have the courage to write about things most people do not admit they even think about."

Whether I decided to show the work or not, or if I just wanted to talk about it, she would be there for me.

One evening, some months later, over a candlelight dinner and two bottles of Chianti, I said, "Even though I feel content, I know there still exists within me a realm where a cruel and beautiful Goddess rules with absolute power. In this place, devotion to Her, not self-esteem, is the ultimate purpose for my life."

Judith looked sad. I felt sorry. I knew she truly cared for me. She did not want to hear that I did not always respect myself. Still, she considered my statement. She would not punish me for being honest.

"Some forms of love thrive in the absence of intimacy," she replied. "We are all creatures of conflict, torn by our attractions and repulsions. Through sex, we come into the world, and the paradoxes of our existence are epitomized by it. I agree that our acts of worship, to be sincere, must come from our deepest, darkest recesses and reflect our life and death concerns. If we had detachment, there would be no heartbreak, but there would be no rapture. The world would be a safer place, but an anticlimactic one. Nevertheless I believe that even though the world is a stage and life is a play, love should not be a toy."

We made love tenderly. Touched by her wisdom and compassion, I slept soundly and woke early. I shook Judith and told her I had made up my mind to let her see the manuscript. She commended me for my bravery.

I went downtown to retrieve the text. When I returned to my apartment I found a note from my Mistress in my mailbox.

I came across one of your old notebooks and read it. Hot stuff, it made me miss my mouse. Will you call me?

Would I?

Taking life one day at a time, I put the letter aside and went back to Judith with the manuscript.

As the elevator lifted me to her floor, devil-may-care, I whispered the prayer.

To You, the Writing in my Flesh, I dedicate myself. Goddess of Love, who brings joy and woe, I am your instrument. My work is not my own but yours.